## An image flashed through Leigh's mind

It was an image of Gabe, beautifully naked. He had his hands on her. Their embrace was beyond intimate. It was so clear, so erotic that Leigh gasped.

"What's wrong?" Gabe glanced around them.

"Nothing," she said on a rush of breath. "A memory, I think."

"Of what?"

She couldn't tell him. Leigh didn't even think she could say the words.

"Was it about us?"

Leigh nodded but didn't offer anything else.

"All right, if you won't answer, I'll fill in the blanks. We had some bad times along with the good ones. *Very* good ones. Yes, we argued, but we always made up. We had all the hopes, dreams and problems of any other couple in love. And yes, damn it, we even had great sex."

He must have sensed that he'd hit upon something. *"Great sex,"* he repeated.

"I won't get involved with you again," she retorted.

"Are you trying to convince me," Gabe drawled, "or yourself?"

Dear Reader,

We have a fabulous fall lineup for you this month and throughout the season, starting with a new Navajo miniseries by Aimée Thurlo called SIGN OF THE GRAY WOLF. Two loners are called to action in the Four Corners area of New Mexico to take care of two women in jeopardy. Look for Daniel "Lightning" Eagle's story in *When Lightning Strikes* and Burke Silentman's next month in *Navajo Justice*.

The explosive CHICAGO CONFIDENTIAL continuity series concludes with Adrianne Lee's *Prince Under Cover.* We just know you are going to love this international story of intrigue and the drama of a royal marriage—to a familiar stranger.... Don't forget: a new Confidential branch will be added to the network next year!

Also this month—another compelling book from newcomer Delores Fossen. In *A Man Worth Remembering,* she reunites an estranged couple after amnesia strikes. Together, can they find the strength to face their enduring love—and find their kidnapped secret child? And can a woman on the edge recover the life and child she lost when she was framed for murder, in Harper Allen's *The Night in Quesiton*? She can if she has the help of the man who put her away.

Pulse pounding, mind-blowing and always breathtaking—that's Harlequin Intrigue.

Enjoy,

Denise O'Sullivan
Associate Senior Editor
Harlequin Intrigue

# A Man Worth Remembering

Delores Fossen

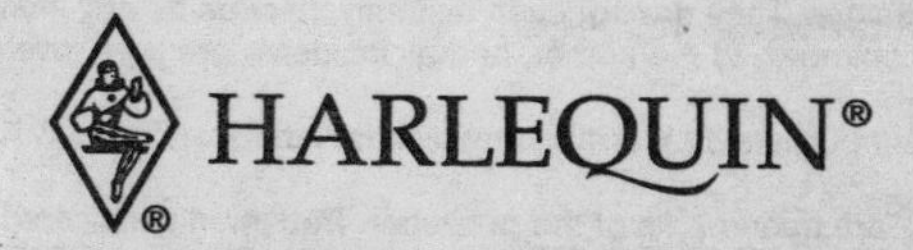


TORONTO • NEW YORK • LONDON
AMSTERDAM • PARIS • SYDNEY • HAMBURG
STOCKHOLM • ATHENS • TOKYO • MILAN • MADRID
PRAGUE • WARSAW • BUDAPEST • AUCKLAND

ISBN 0-373-22679-9

A MAN WORTH REMEMBERING



This edition published by arrangement with Harlequin Books S.A.



Visit us at www.eHarlequin.com

**Printed in U.S.A.**

## ABOUT THE AUTHOR

Imagine a family tree that includes Texas cowboys, Choctaw and Cherokee Indians, a Louisiana pirate and a Scottish rebel who battled side by side with William Wallace. With ancestors like that, it's easy to understand why Texas author and former air force captain Delores Fossen feels as if she was genetically predisposed to writing romances. Along the way to fulfilling her DNA destiny, Delores married an air force Top Gun who just happens to be of Viking descent. With all those romantic bases covered, she doesn't have to look too far for inspiration.

**Books by Delores Fossen**

HARLEQUIN INTRIGUE

648—HIS CHILD
679—A MAN WORTH REMEMBERING

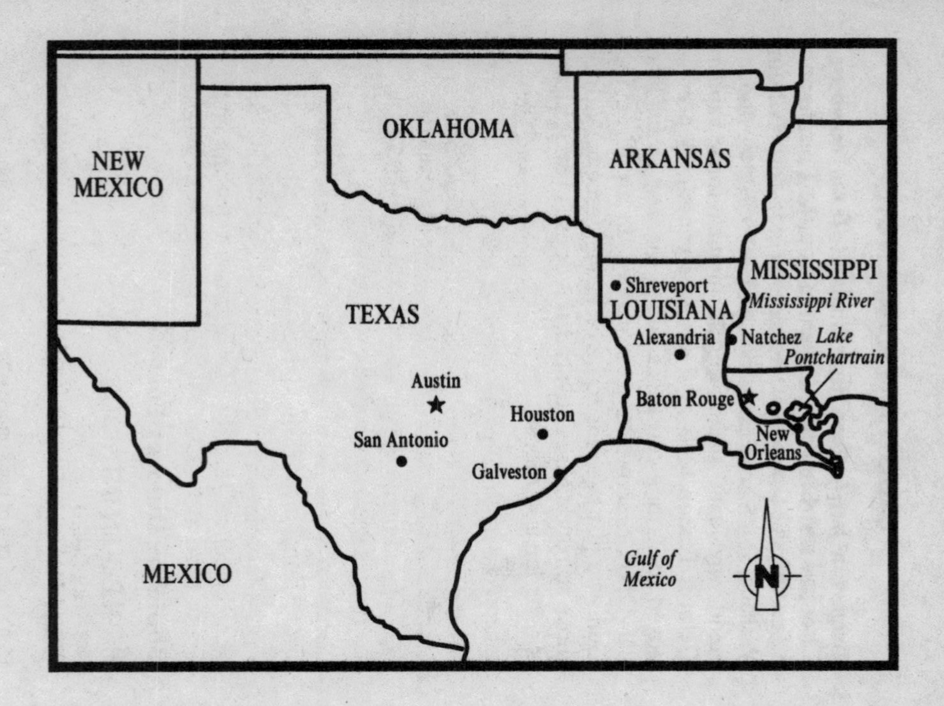
NEW MEXICO
OKLAHOMA
ARKANSAS
MISSISSIPPI
Mississippi River
Shreveport
LOUISIANA
TEXAS
Alexandria
Natchez
Lake Pontchartrain
Austin
Baton Rouge
Houston
San Antonio
New Orleans
Galveston
MEXICO
Gulf of Mexico
N

## CAST OF CHARACTERS

***Leigh O'Brien***—Even though she's lost her memory, Leigh senses that she and her husband, Gabe, once had a life and love that's worth remembering. Without realizing she has a secret that can destroy the new bonds between them, Leigh places her life, and her heart, in Gabe's hands.

***Special Agent Gabe Sanchez***—Gabe vows to do his job and protect his estranged wife from a killer, but he doesn't want to give Leigh another chance to crush his heart. Too bad he can't forget the love they once shared—a love that is threatened when Gabe learns the truth Leigh has kept from him.

***Wade Jenkins***—A key member of the task force assembled to protect Leigh and catch the killer. But is Wade someone Leigh and Gabe can trust? Or is he the very man who wants Leigh dead?

***Teresa Walters***—An ATF agent with more than a professional interest in Gabe.

***Frank Templeton***—Leigh's former assistant on the FBI's Evidence Response Team. Does someone want Frank dead as well, or is he the mastermind behind the plot to kill Leigh?

To my sister, Linda Reeves,
who taught me many of life's most important lessons.

# *Chapter One*

Leigh realized she was being murdered.

She regained consciousness in the water. Cold, deep, dark water. It was above her, beneath her, around her on all sides. Smothering her.

Terror shot through her. She frantically tried to swim but couldn't. Her hands and feet were tied together. Water gushed into her nose and mouth. Her throat clenched. It hurt. She hurt. Her chest pounded as if it might shatter.

Someone had put her there. But who? She could just make out a milky image on the bridge above the water's surface. No face. No name. Just someone who obviously wanted her dead.

Inch by excruciating inch, she sank lower. She fought against the urge to surrender, to close her eyes and just give up so the pain would stop. No. She wouldn't give up. Couldn't. God, she didn't want to die.

Leigh twisted her body, using the last of her breath to try to stop her downward slide. She didn't succeed.

The water coiled around her and sent her into a dizzying spiral until her feet dipped into the clotted mud at the bottom.

She didn't see the man before his arm snaked around her waist, but she felt his firm grip. It was a lifeline. Hope. Right now, hope and this man were all she had.

He stopped the mud from swallowing her up and began to haul her toward the surface. Leigh tried to help, but her wrists and feet were still bound. No matter how hard she struggled, she couldn't free herself.

Somehow, he got them out of the water, dragging her onto a muddy embankment. And then he kissed her. At least she thought that's what he was doing until she felt the air gust into her mouth. No. Not a kiss. Mouth-to-mouth resuscitation.

"It's okay," the man said. "You'll be all right."

He knelt beside her, his movements jerky but somehow controlled, and he got the ropes off her hands and feet. Every few seconds, his gaze darted around them as if he was watching for something.

Not something, she realized.

Someone.

After all, the person who'd try to kill her could return to finish the job.

She didn't have time to react to that terrifying realization. Her teeth began to chatter. Her body shook. She was cold and wet, and her head throbbed in pain. For that matter, the rest of her throbbed, too. But at least she was alive. Because of this man, she was alive. Too bad she didn't have enough breath to thank him.

He leaned over her to examine her forehead. It was dusk, but what was left of the filmy sunlight allowed her to see him and his resolute expression. Did she know him?

No.

He was a stranger.

"You saved my life," she managed to say.

Water slipped off him and splattered onto her face. With the same gentle touch he'd used on her forehead, he wiped away the drops, letting his fingertips linger on her cheek.

"Yes. I did." He mumbled something else under his breath. Something in Spanish. And he shook his head. "I'd still like to have your butt for what you pulled, but we can get into all of that later."

She didn't understand what he meant. Exactly what had she *pulled?* She hadn't asked to be in that water. Had she? No, she was sure of that. This was no suicide attempt. She'd fought to stay alive.

"Who are you?" she asked.

Something she couldn't distinguish rifled through his eyes. "What the devil do you mean by that?"

"I'd like to know your name," she clarified.

He sat back on his heels and glared down at her. "Just what kind of sick game are you playing, huh?" She barely got out a denying shake of her head before he continued. "Believe me, it won't work." With each word he got louder. "I want answers. I *deserve* answers."

"I'd like some answers, too. For starters, please tell me who you are."

"Gabe," he said, hissing it out like profanity. "But you know that."

No, she didn't. She shoved her fingers through her hair to push the wet strands out of her eyes. Part of her thought she might recognize his name, the way he'd said it, but she couldn't be sure. Mercy, if her head would just stop pounding, maybe she could sort through all of this.

"Gabe Sanchez," he added after a moment.

Still nothing. But she *should* know him. Maybe she felt that because of his formidable expression and not because of any true recollection. "Well, thank you, Mr. Sanchez, for saving me. I thought I was going to die."

He sat there as drops of water slid down his face. He seemed oblivious to the water, to his drenched clothes. Oblivious to everything around them. Everything but her. He stared craters in her.

"You would have died if I hadn't been here," he assured her. "Someone shot you. When that didn't work, they clubbed you and threw you in the lake."

She gasped, horrified that someone would do such terrible things to her. "Someone shot me?"

"Looks that way. It's just a graze, but combined with that lump, you'll probably have one heck of a headache."

She nodded. She already had one heck of a headache so there was no *probably* about it.

"Who did this to you?" he demanded. "Who tried to kill you?"

He seemed angry with her, and she didn't know why. Worse, she didn't know why things didn't make sense. Who had done this to her? Why had she been in the water? And who was this stranger who expected her to have all the answers?

"I don't know." She touched her forehead. When she drew back her hand, she noticed the watery blood on her fingertips. She was injured but didn't even remember how it'd happened. God, how could she possibly not know that? "Did you see anyone before you jumped in after me?"

"Just a car speeding away. I couldn't make out the license plate." Vigilantly, he looked around them again. "When I saw the air bubbles in the water, I dived in."

Thank God he had. If not, she would without a doubt be dead. "Where are we?"

"Lake Pontchartrain." His narrowed gaze came back to her. "Are you trying to make me believe you really don't know?"

She glanced around her. All she saw was the sun setting on an ordinary lake. Other than that, it didn't look familiar. "Are we near Houston?"

"Houston?" he spat out. "We're just outside New Orleans."

Sweet heaven. Even with a multiple choice, she

wouldn't have gotten it right. What the heck was she doing here?

"You honestly don't remember?" he asked.

"No." It was the one answer of which she was certain.

"All right, let's try something easy. What's the date?"

Again, she tried to concentrate. "Is it June something?"

He blew out a long breath. "Not quite. It's August twelfth. Okay. Here's a question that nobody gets wrong. What's your name?"

She opened her mouth, but nothing came out. Absolutely nothing. Her mind was a complete blank.

He stilled, his expression registering more than a little alarm. "You don't know your own name?"

She shook her head, trying to will away the dizziness that started to overpower her. "I have no idea." And she didn't. No idea whatsoever.

She was ready to panic, when it occurred to her that this had to be a dream. Yes, a dream. It was the only logical explanation. A full-fledged, mind-blowing nightmare. All she had to do was wake up, and she'd remember everything. Heck, right now she probably wasn't anywhere near this lake but in her own bed at home.

Wherever home was.

She blinked hard several times, trying to force a different scene to appear in front of her, but the nightmare was still there. And so was Gabe Sanchez. He stared at her, his dark, suspicious eyes filled with questions that she knew she couldn't answer.

So, with the taste of the muddy lake still in her mouth, she closed her eyes and let the dream take over.

VOICES WOKE HER. She caught a word here and there, but much of what she heard didn't make sense. Philip. Frank Templeton. Sanchez.

Gabe Sanchez.

The man who saved her. There were at least two other voices: a male and a female. All three used hushed tones, but they seemed to be arguing.

She forced her eyes open, even though the overhead fluorescent lights made her wince, and pain stabbed through her head. She felt groggy, almost drunk, but she finally managed to see the trio near the doorway. Sanchez, an attractive woman with pinned-up dark hair and a tall blond man.

The woman and the other man wore business suits in neutral colors. No suit for Sanchez. He had on faded jeans, a plain white T-shirt and a shoulder holster that had a pistol sticking out of it. There was a beeper attached to his belt loop.

She glanced down at her own clothes. Someone had dressed her in drab green surgical scrubs. And she was on a gurney.

"I'm not in ICU," she said to herself. "Or in an emergency room."

It looked more like a huge supply closet. There were

several metal shelves crammed with boxes. A single window graced the far wall, and the blinds were closed, so she couldn't tell if it was night or day. Or if it was covered with bars. She was afraid it might have bars.

"It's what you have to tell her," the woman insisted.

Sanchez shook his head. "I won't."

The woman folded her arms over her chest and tapped her foot. "It wasn't a request. Now, what part of it didn't you understand?"

"The part where you started spouting Justice Department garbage, that's when, Teresa."

"You'd rather have her dead? Because that's what'll happen. Heck, it almost did, or have you forgotten that already?"

"I haven't forgotten anything. I'm the one who pulled her out of that lake." Sanchez mumbled something under his breath. Leigh only caught the *Jesucristo* part. "Hell, she almost died in my arms."

She lifted her head off the gurney. "Who are you people?"

The three rifled their gazes toward her, but they didn't say anything. She studied each one, trying to interpret their expressions and the snippets of conversation she'd heard.

She definitely didn't trust the blond man, and yet she couldn't say why. The woman was no ally either. She didn't know what to make of Sanchez, but since he'd saved her from drowning, she would cast her lot with him if it came down to choosing sides.

It would, she feared, come down to choosing sides.

"Better yet," she amended when none of them answered her, "who am I?"

Gabe Sanchez walked toward her with an almost graceful ease. He was tall, over six feet, and muscular. His biceps strained against the cotton T-shirt. He had chocolate-colored hair that was short and neat. Efficient. Low maintenance.

When he got closer, she saw that his eyes were a deep blue. They, too, seemed efficient—his gaze swept over her with a minimal amount of effort. However, she had no doubt that he'd just given her the once-over.

The others trailed behind Sanchez, stopping when he did. They were friends. No, more than that. Or less than that. Maybe much, much less.

God, why was it so hard to figure out things?

"You still don't remember who you are?" Sanchez asked her.

"No. Why is that? What's wrong with me?"

"You took a hard hit on the head. It might take a while for everything to come back."

She touched the bandage on her forehead. There was indeed a lump under the gauze swatch, but she hadn't needed to feel it to know it was there. That was no doubt the source of her vicious headache.

"I have a concussion?" she asked.

Sanchez nodded. "And a few stitches in your forehead and on your ankle where the rope abraded your skin. The doctor examined you, but he doesn't think your memory loss has anything to do with the head injury. In other words, no brain damage. He said it was brought on by emotional trauma.''

''Disassociative amnesia,'' she softly added. ''How long will it last?'' But she already knew. Like her aversion to the blond man and the woman, she just didn't know how she knew it.

It was Sanchez who answered. ''The doctor's not sure. It could be hours. Or days.''

''Or I might never regain my memory,'' she provided.

She lowered her head and tried to absorb that. She couldn't. It was impossible to understand anything while her thoughts whirled around like a tornado.

God, what she was going to do? She didn't know who she was, not her name, not her age. Nothing. She didn't know if she was still in danger or if she could trust anyone. She didn't even know what these people had to do with her.

But they knew.

They likely knew everything about her.

''What's my name?'' she asked Sanchez. She wanted answers, and by God, she wanted them now.

''Leigh O'Brien.''

That didn't mean anything to her. Only the water and Sanchez saving her meant anything. For all practical purposes, her life had begun the moment she realized she was drowning. That wasn't a comforting thought. "Where am I?"

"A private clinic near New Orleans."

So, they hadn't left the area. But it wasn't an ordinary clinic. She was sure of that. "Are you a cop?"

"No."

"Am *I* a cop?"

The room went deadly silent. "No," the blond man finally answered.

Leigh didn't like that hesitation. It sent a wave of panic through her. "Am I a criminal then?" And she braced herself for the answer.

These people might be here to arrest her for something she'd done wrong. Had someone tossed her in that lake because of a drug deal gone bad? An organized-crime housecleaning? What awful thing had she done to make someone want to murder her?

The blond man took a step forward, placing himself slightly ahead of the others. "You're not a criminal."

She allowed herself a short breath of relief. Just one. And got down to business. "Since these questions could go on forever, why don't you just tell me who you are?"

The three glanced at each other before the blond man said anything else. "I'm Wade Jenkins. People call me Jinx. Special Agent Sanchez and I are with the FBI. Agent Teresa Walters is an agent with the Bureau of Alcohol, Tobacco and Firearms—the ATF."

"FBI. ATF," Leigh repeated. "What about me? Am I some sort of agent, too?"

"You're a concerned citizen." The blond man burrowed his index finger into his eyebrow. "A concerned citizen with a rather large problem."

"Obviously," Leigh snapped. "Believe me, after everything that's happened, I can guess there's a problem. Now, other than a concerned citizen, who am I? If I don't work for an agency with initials, where do I work?"

"At a bookstore in Austin, Texas," Jinx answered.

"A bookstore?" A *bookstore.* That couldn't be right. Nothing about that felt right.

He didn't elaborate. "Exactly what do you remember about being in the water?"

A good question. Too bad she didn't have a good answer. "Not much other than Agent Sanchez saving me. Before that, all I remember is struggling and sinking deeper."

"Any idea who put you in the lake?"

She tried to force the answer to appear in her mind. It didn't work. She had no more answers about that now than she had when Sanchez had first asked her. "No. I have an image of someone on a bridge, but I can't make out any of the features. Someone wearing light colors. I don't suppose that helps you any?"

"No," Teresa Walters answered in a frustrated huff. "But your amnesia is only part of the problem. This might not be over. Someone might make another attempt to kill you."

Leigh swallowed hard. She hadn't considered that. Yet. However, after her adrenaline fatigue wore off, it would no doubt have occurred to her. Amnesia or not, she still had common sense.

She hoped.

Leigh turned her gaze to Sanchez. "Who wants me dead?"

He lifted his shoulder. "We don't know."

"Can you at least tell me what it involves? What—"

"The less you know, the better," Jinx interrupted.

"Maybe that's your way of looking at it, but I see things from a little different perspective than you do. Someone tried to kill me, and I think I have a right to know why."

"Jinx is right about this, Leigh," Sanchez spoke up. "Even if we told you everything, it wouldn't make you safer. That's why we'll provide you with protection."

She shook her head, already objecting. "Now, wait a minute. I don't even know any of you, and you want me to place my life in your hands? How do I know you're not the people who tried to kill me, huh?"

"That doesn't make any sense," Sanchez answered. "If we wanted you dead, I wouldn't have pulled you out of that lake."

"But those two didn't pull me out." She pointed to Wade Jenkins and then to Teresa Walters. "The way I see it, I'm in a real mess here. What if some secret's trapped in my head, and you want me around just long enough to get it? What if you kill me the minute I tell you what you want to know?''

Agent Walters threw her hands in the air. ''I give up. Let me know when you can talk some sense into her.''

Leigh was about to tell the woman exactly what she thought of her when Sanchez broke in. ''You can trust me, Leigh.'' The offer had not come effortlessly. It came with a scalpel-sharp glare.

''Why? Because you saved my life?''

He didn't answer, but after a moment Jinx did. ''Not just that. You can trust him because Gabe Sanchez is your husband.''

## *Chapter Two*

Gabe could almost feel her gaze crawl all over him. He braced himself for the storm he was about to face. And there would be one heck of a storm when Leigh got going with her questions. No doubt about it.

"My husband?" she repeated.

He nodded but didn't add more than that. The details of their marital status were among a mile-long list of things he didn't want to discuss with her. Too bad he'd probably have to do just that before this was over.

"Is it true?" she asked. "Are we really married?"

He eased onto the edge of the narrow gurney and stared down at her. No sense standing for what would basically be an interrogation. "I'll answer that if you'll tell me the truth. Is this memory loss all an act?"

"No." Aggravation danced across her eyes. "I wish it were, because I can promise you I wouldn't be here. I don't like being here."

"Yeah, I know what you mean." Gabe made a sweeping glance around the room. "I don't care much for it myself."

Leigh made the same sweeping glance, and when she finished, their eyes met, coming together until they held. "Are you really my husband?"

Well, this was one part of the conversation that he obviously couldn't put off. Not that it surprised him. If their situations were reversed, he'd want to know the same thing. "Afraid so. You're not happy about that?"

"The jury's still out. It's hard to know if I'm happy about it when I don't even know you. So, how long have we been married?"

Ah, a test. He'd expected that, too. "Four years, six months." He paused, thinking. "And eighteen days."

He could have given her the hours if she'd asked. Gabe cursed himself. It didn't please him that he could recall something so painful in such detail.

"That long," she mumbled.

Yeah, that long. But half of that time she'd been gone. Now, here she was—right back in his life. It had taken him too long to get over her the last time. She'd turned him upside down and hung him out to dry. He didn't want another dose of that.

Even with the dye job, she hadn't changed much. A little thinner. And maybe there was something different about her expression. The old Leigh had been so self-assured. Not now though. There was a good reason for that. After all, someone had tried to kill her. That murder attempt no doubt had something to do with what had brought her back to him. Fate working overtime again.

Sometimes fate didn't know which end was up.

Well, he wasn't about to buy into anything that dealt with fate.

She continued to stare at him as if sizing him up. "Why didn't you say something earlier about being my husband?"

"There wasn't time. You were unconscious when I brought you here." He knew that wouldn't be the last of her questions, and he didn't have to wait long for her to verify that.

Leigh glanced at his hand. "Why isn't either of us wearing a wedding ring?"

Hell. The woman could certainly open old wounds. Gabe pulled the neck chain out of his T-shirt so she could see the simple gold band that it held. "I'm left-handed, and it catches on the holster. I'm not sure where your ring is. Maybe it slipped off in the lake."

Or maybe she'd thrown it away. He wouldn't put it past her. Obviously their marriage vows hadn't meant much to her. He couldn't say the same. And that was probably the only explanation he had for why he still wore his wedding ring. One thing was for sure, as soon as he got out of there, he planned to get rid of it. It was something he should have done months ago.

"I have to go," Jinx announced, the sound of his voice slicing through the heavy silence. "I need to update a few people about what's happened and try to figure out what we're going to do. Gabe, you wait here with Leigh."

Of course. Gabe hadn't expected it to be any other way.

"I should head out, too," Agent Walters added after checking her watch. She gave Gabe's sleeve a tug. "No improvising, all right?"

Gabe didn't concur either verbally or otherwise. Nor did he disagree with the woman who was coleader of this so-called task force. He just kept his rebellious thoughts to himself. "I'll walk you two out." He stood and looked down at Leigh. "Stay put."

Her unbandaged eyebrow winged up. "Do I have a choice?"

"No," he clarified over his shoulder.

"I told you to be nice to her," Jinx said the moment they were outside the door. "I told you to gain her trust."

Gabe wanted to laugh. "I don't perform miracles."

"No, but you will do your job."

Jinx's words hit him like a heavyweight's fist, even though Gabe had tried to brace himself for it. "And what exactly do you mean by that?"

"It means you'll protect her until we can make other arrangements." There was no hesitation in Jinx's tone, and that tone drew a clear line between their friendship and his role as Gabe's boss.

Gabe scrubbed his hand over his face. "It means you want me to be her bodyguard."

"If necessary," Teresa piped in. Jinx gave a nod of agreement.

It would be necessary. No doubt about it. That was

the only way Gabe could see this playing out. Heck, if he hadn't been on the receiving end of this assignment, he might have even considered it a good idea.

There were just a couple of problems with this particular plan that Jinx and Teresa had come up with for him. It would mean he'd have to spend a lot of time with his wife. A wife he didn't want. A wife who didn't want him. But she was also a vulnerable woman with a killer after her.

Hell.

He'd do what the Justice Department wanted him to do, and then he was out of there. Leigh could go back to whatever the hell she'd been doing, and he would get on with his life. All he had to do was keep her alive, catch the bad guy and leave. Especially, leave.

There was no way he'd allow himself to be drawn back into her life. No way.

LEIGH WAITED until Sanchez and the others walked out of the room. "Stay put," she said, repeating the terse order he'd just given her. "As if I had a choice."

In fact, her choices were extremely limited. Possibly even nil. She had amnesia, was hurt and didn't know where she could go to get out of danger. That didn't mean she trusted the three people who'd just left the room. Or that she believed them. She was almost positive they hadn't told her the truth.

*It's what you have to tell her,* Agent Teresa Walters had said before they knew she was awake. People didn't usually make remarks like that if they planned to tell the truth.

The whole truth, anyway.

So just what did the others want Sanchez to keep from her? She certainly intended to find out.

Realizing that she had to go to the bathroom, Leigh tossed back the covers and swung her legs off the gurney. She was achy, and her vision was spotty. There was a thick white bandage completely encircling her right ankle, and when she stood, the stitches pinched.

She made use of a pair of green flip-flops that were under the gurney and went in search of the bathroom. It wasn't hard to find. It was the only door other than the one through which her fearless protectors had exited.

The bathroom was enormous and had two vats filled with dirty linen and hospital-style gowns. The laundry chute was as wide as the bins, indicating the need to send plenty of soiled clothing to the laundry room. A regular clinic probably wouldn't have such a need.

So just what was this place?

Since she hadn't heard any traffic or sounds normally associated with a clinic, it was probably some secured area. Perhaps a military installation or maybe a safe house used by the FBI.

Now, just what did the FBI and an ATF agent want with a bookstore employee from Austin? Perhaps the books in the store weren't the run-of-the-mill variety. If so, she was obviously more than just a concerned citizen.

Leigh put that thought on the back burner when she noticed the mirror above the sink. She approached it cautiously, afraid of what she might see in her own reflection. And equally afraid of what she might *not* see.

Disappointment soon replaced the cautiousness. She didn't recognize a thing about herself. The face of a stranger stared back at her.

A troubled stranger.

Almost frantically, she studied her face harder, trying to force herself to see something familiar. She was pale and wondered if it was from the trauma or if that was her usual coloring. Perhaps a combination of both.

The skin surrounding the bandage was bruised—the purplish stain bled down to her cheekbone where someone had obviously hit her pretty hard. A blunt object was her guess.

Her features weren't prominent. Average. She certainly wasn't beautiful. Her hair was chin-length and cedar-colored, but since her roots were light brown, she figured that she wasn't a natural redhead. She checked in the most obvious place to verify her conclusion, stretching out the waist of the scrubs to look inside.

No. She wasn't a redhead.

She leaned closer to the mirror, suddenly puzzled by her eyes. They weren't the same color. One was dark brown; the other, pale green. She automatically reached toward the brown eye and removed the colored contact that had camouflaged her iris. So, her eyes were really green, and since she could see perfectly without the contact, she had to believe she'd worn them for cosmetic reasons.

Why?

Colored contacts. Dyed hair. She'd disguised her appearance. It made sense. Perhaps she'd been hiding because someone wanted her dead. Too bad the disguise hadn't worked. Obviously, someone had seen right through it and gone after her.

Leigh noticed the scar then. A puckered dimple on her right forearm. It appeared to be well healed, but she thought it might be a bullet wound. Or maybe her imagination was just working overtime. Just the sight of the injury, however, caused a sickening feeling in her stomach. It was yet another chilling reminder of her past she couldn't remember.

She finished up in the bathroom, returned to the room and got back on the gurney. A moment later, Gabe pushed opened the door and came in with a large disposable cup in each hand.

"Coffee," he announced. "I figured you'd need your caffeine fix by now."

Leigh didn't know about that, but the steamy brew smelled wonderful. "I'm a big coffee drinker?"

He nodded and glanced at one cup and then the other, apparently trying to decide which one was hers. He finally took a sip from one and grimaced. "Yours. Three sugars, just the way you like it."

She took the cup, knowing she would indeed like

it. Odd. Why had sugary coffee felt familiar and not her husband?

*Her husband.*

As she'd done to her own face in the mirror, Leigh scrutinized his. Actually, he wasn't bad-looking. A little on the rough side, and the small scar on his chin only contributed to that image. His skin was a pale bronze, obviously a DNA contribution from the Hispanic heritage that his surname signified. The dark blue eyes, however, indicated some Anglo blood as well. All in all, it was a good mix that had produced an interesting face.

His eyes were...not bedroom eyes, even though it was the first description that sprang to mind. The dark lashes made them look half-closed, dreamy, but there was nothing *bedroom* about them. Those eyes meant business.

"Is the coffee all right?" Gabe asked when she took a sip.

"It's fine. So, you know how I like my coffee—that still doesn't mean I believe everything you've told me." Placing her cup on the table beside his, she glanced at her ring finger and noticed a faint line. Not necessarily from a wedding band. But it was possible. "Did I have any ID on me when you pulled me out of the lake?"

He stretched out his leg so he could work his fingers into the front pocket of his jeans. He fished out a single key. "This was tucked under the floor mat in the car. It had your fingerprints on it."

"It's for a car?"

Sanchez shook his head. "You left the keys to your rental car in the ignition. This looks more like a house key. Is it familiar?"

"No." It looked like a key, that's all. A key to a house, and she had no idea where that house might be. Austin, maybe, since that's where she supposedly worked. "You didn't find a purse or wallet on me or in the car?"

"I think the person who tried to kill you probably took it."

That was possible, which made her wonder if the attack was robbery related. But she didn't think so. She probably wouldn't be here if it'd been a simple robbery.

Leigh glanced at him. So far, he'd cooperated with her questions. Well, some of them anyway, but she had no way of knowing if what he'd told her was the truth or even part of the truth. Heck, she wasn't even convinced that the man was truly her husband.

"Why didn't you kiss me when you pulled me out of the water?" she asked. "If we're really married, wouldn't a kiss have been the husbandly thing to do?"

It happened so quickly, she didn't have time to protest or wonder why she'd issued such a stupid invitation in the first place. Gabe slipped his hand around the back of her neck and angled her head. His mouth came to hers. Touched. Brushed. And lingered.

Before he got down to business.

The kiss that followed was hot and clever. Slightly

rough and a heck of a lot longer than it should have been. It certainly wasn't a husbandly peck. It had a slick veneer of all sorts of emotion, including some anger, but that didn't quite cover up the pure, raw attraction that sizzled beneath.

When he finally set her free, there was no doubt in Leigh's mind that she'd been kissed by someone who knew exactly how to do it.

Gabe looked deeply into her eyes. "Remember me now, *mi vida?*" he drawled, his tone a cocky challenge.

Actually, Leigh didn't, but she thought she might *like* to remember him. Too bad that kiss muddled her brain even more than it already was.

She pushed him away and turned her head toward the window. There wasn't much she could do about her erratic breathing, but she didn't want him to see the telltale bewilderment that had to be in her eyes.

"Look, I may not know who I am, but I'm not stupid," Leigh said crisply. "Other than the obvious thing of someone trying to kill me, something isn't right."

"Funny, it felt right to me." When her gaze came to his, he rubbed the pad of his thumb over his bottom lip and flashed her a grin that set her teeth on edge.

"I didn't mean that kiss. There has to be a reason why I have all these crazy feelings." Leigh aimed her finger at him when Gabe started to speak. "And I'm not talking about your mouth on mine. Why won't you tell me what's really going on here?"

Gabe dropped onto the gurney right next to her. "You'll be safer not knowing."

"I didn't buy that from Jinx, and I won't buy it from you. I could regain my memory in the next minute, and if I follow through with that asinine theory, I'll be in more danger than I am right now. Somebody wants me dead, and I don't think they care if I have amnesia or not."

He nodded eventually. "Okay. I'll give you the condensed version."

"Why not the whole thing?"

"It'll only muddy the waters, and it won't help you sort things out." He didn't wait for her to agree. "A little over two years ago you came across some sensitive information regarding a high-ranking government official named Joe Dayton."

Leigh gave that some thought. All right. What he said could be true. "I found this when I was working at the bookstore in Austin?"

The corner of Gabe's mouth kicked up. "No, you were working somewhere else at the time. And don't bother to ask where, because I won't tell you."

"Another of Jinx's orders, or did that come from Special Agent Walters?"

"Not Jinx. Not Teresa. *My* order. Like I said, it'll only confuse you more if I overload you with a bunch of facts that you don't need right now."

Leigh wasn't happy about it, but she'd take what she could get. Besides, on that point he might be right.

"Okay, finish the short version. What about this Joe Dayton?"

"He was as dirty as they come," he answered after hesitating. "We didn't know if he was working alone or if what you learned would make you a target."

She shook her head, not understanding. "So, why did he wait two years to come after me?"

"You've been hiding all this time."

Finally, something made sense. But it was just the beginning. She needed a lot more pieces of information for this puzzle to come together.

Gabe's pager began to beep. He jabbed the button to make the sound stop and sprang to his feet. In the same motion, he whipped out his pistol and reeled toward the door.

Leigh hadn't thought she could be any more frightened, but that did it. Her heart began to pound. "What's wrong?" she asked, getting off the gurney.

Gabe motioned toward the window. "See if anyone's out there."

She hobbled toward it, ignoring her stitches, and peeked through the side of the blinds. It was dark, and they were several floors off the ground, but she saw six cars in the parking lot.

"Nobody," she reported. But the words hardly left her mouth when four men exited one of the cars. "Somebody," she amended. "There are four of them."

"Watch the door," Gabe ordered and then traded places with her so he could glance out the window.

''We don't have much time. We have to get out of here.''

Leigh started out the door, but Gabe latched onto her arm and yanked her back. ''We can't go that way.''

''You're not suggesting we use the window?''

''No. They probably left someone to take care of us if we try that.''

That was a chilling thought. *Take care of us.* In other words, kill them. ''So, how do we get out?''

He didn't answer. Gabe grabbed a box from one of the shelves and pulled out another gun. It looked even more deadly than the one he already had. He checked to make sure it was loaded. It was. And he thrust it into her hands.

''What—'' But Leigh didn't get a chance to protest. Gabe shoved open the bathroom door, pulling her inside with him. He held open the laundry hatch with his elbow and swung his leg into the opening.

''I'm going down first,'' he told her. ''Count to ten and follow me unless you hear gunfire. If that happens, barricade yourself in here and shoot anyone who comes through that door. And I mean anyone. Understand?''

She nodded and examined the gun. ''Do I know how to use this?''

''You know.'' He climbed into the duct. ''Now, let's hope you remember.''

Leigh hoped the same thing. ''Let me guess—I learned how to fire guns like this at the bookstore?''

Gabe flashed her a dry grin and ignored her question. ‘‘There’s no safety on that piece. If necessary, aim and fire. And Leigh? This time do as I tell you.’’

Before she could ask what he meant by that, he let himself drop. She kept her gaze on him until he disappeared into the tunnel.

‘‘One,’’ Leigh counted.

She stood there for a few panicky seconds, wondering again if she should trust him. And wondering if she should follow him. She really had no reason to trust him, but she wouldn’t have any reason to trust those four men about to come through the door either. They no doubt wanted to kill her. She didn’t know for sure what Gabe wanted to do with her.

So this was the proverbial rock and a hard place?

‘‘Ten,’’ she mumbled when she heard hurried footsteps in the hallway on the other side of the wall.

She climbed into the laundry hatch and let herself go. Moments later, she heard gunshots, but it was too late to stop her downward slide. Or anything else for that matter.

She was headed straight toward those deadly-sounding shots, and there was nothing she could do about it.

# Chapter Three

Leigh saw Gabe just before she reached the bottom—a split-second glimpse of a man prepared to kill. He was behind a concrete post about fifteen feet from the laundry chute. He'd assumed a classic isosceles stance with a two-handed grip on his pistol. Every inch of him looked primed to fight.

"Take cover!" Gabe yelled. Someone punctuated his command with a spray of bullets.

She torpedoed out of the chute, quickly rolled over the side of the bin and dropped. She landed in an unladylike sprawl on the concrete floor.

"I said take cover. Now!" Gabe yelled.

She was certainly trying to do that. Unfortunately, her body didn't want to cooperate. Leigh scrambled to her feet and with her flip-flops smacking against the floor, she ducked behind another of those concrete posts.

Should she try to get to Gabe? she wondered. Even with the obvious danger of someone shooting at them, she still considered the idea. It seemed a better option than being on her own when she didn't know what to do.

The next bullets that strafed across the floor put a stop to that notion. She had to stay put.

From her position, she couldn't see Gabe. There were more laundry bins, huge washing machines, industrial-size dryers and rows of metal tables. From the narrow view that she had, there were many places a gunman could hide.

Too many.

Besides, she didn't even know if there was just *one* gunman. She'd seen four men in the parking lot, and it was entirely possible all four were somewhere in the room, waiting for her to make a mistake.

If she called out to Gabe to ask him what to do, she might give away her position and force him to give away his. He probably wouldn't appreciate that. Sweet heaven. Another rock and a hard place.

"I'll take that," the man snarled. He snatched the gun from her hand and pressed it to her head.

Not Gabe. Someone else. One of the gunmen, no doubt. How the heck had he gotten so close? Leigh hadn't heard a thing. Of course, her heart was pounding so loudly, she was practically deaf.

Relying purely on instinct, she stabbed her elbow into the man's stomach and quickly spun around. Leigh used all her strength and rammed the heel of her right hand into his Adam's apple. She followed it with a left-handed jab to his mouth. He hissed and staggered back.

Leigh saw him clearly then. Too clearly. He was most certainly one of the men from the parking lot. There was no expression in his muddy-colored eyes, no emotion on his face. He latched onto her neck and roughly twisted her so her back was against his chest.

"Quit fighting me," he warned, shoving the gun even harder to her temple.

His voice was raspy, apparently from the blow she'd managed to deliver to his throat. That didn't give her much satisfaction. He towered over her. And he was solid. He could easily kill her with his bare hands. Of course, he wouldn't have to do something so menial since he had her gun and probably his as well.

"Let's do this the right way," the man yelled across the room to Gabe. "Depending on what you do, I can make this easy for her, or I can make it real slow and ugly."

Leigh didn't care much for those two choices. The man was no doubt talking about how he intended to kill her. "Step out where I can see you, Agent Sanchez," he ordered.

She wasn't sure what Gabe would do. Until she heard the thud of his weapon drop to the floor. He stepped out from behind the post and walked toward them with his hands tucked behind his head.

God. He was surrendering.

Her heart started to pound harder. She'd hoped he might be able to save them or at least buy some time so she could figure out what to do. But Gabe hadn't done that. Instead, he'd surrendered to a man who would probably kill them both before she drew her next breath.

"Who are you working for?" Gabe asked him.

"No one who's willing to bargain with you."

"Then how about we bargain? Before you say no, I think you should know the woman you're holding has plenty of money. I'm sure we can work out some financial arrangements that'd make it profitable for you to let her go."

"Save your breath," the man retorted. "I've got no plans to be a rich dead man, and that's what'll happen if I cut a deal with the likes of you."

Her gaze connected with Gabe's. There was a slight lift to his right eyebrow. For the first time, she recognized something in his eyes. Exactly *what,* she couldn't say, but he was definitely trying to communicate.

In a move that seemed both in slow motion and at a speed not humanly possible, Gabe's left hand whipped out from behind his head. He held another gun that he'd hidden. Something small and sleek. The fluorescent light licked the silvery metal and sent a flash across Leigh's face. Gabe aimed the gun directly at her.

She had no time to think, no time to react. She briefly, very briefly, considered that Gabe and his gun would be the last things she'd ever see. But what she couldn't figure out was why he wanted her dead, especially after he had saved her.

Gabe double-tapped the trigger. The shots cracked

like enormous wads of chewing gum. Leigh felt warm spatters of blood on her cheek and waited for the pain or numbness to follow what was certainly a fatal head wound.

That didn't happen.

Instead, the man behind her slumped into a heap, the pistol he'd held against her temple clattering to the floor.

Her breath shattered, a noise coming from deep within her throat. Leigh's hands began to shake violently. Still, she kept her attention focused on Gabe, afraid to blink for fear he'd disappear before she could get to him.

Getting to him, she soon learned, wasn't even necessary. It seemed he made it to her in one step. She grabbed onto him and held tight.

Without breaking her grip, Gabe picked up the gun he'd tossed on the floor and placed the smaller one into the slide holster on the back waist of his jeans. He handed Leigh the other weapon that the man had taken from her.

"There's no need for you to see that," he said, referring to the body. He led her toward the door.

He was right. There was no need for her to see the man. That didn't stop Leigh from glancing back at the lifeless body and the perfectly centered hole in his head. Gabe had literally shot the man right between the eyes. The other bullet wound was only a fraction of an inch above the first one.

She pressed her hand to her stomach, hoping she didn't get sick. "He's dead?" she asked unnecessarily.

"He's dead."

"You could have shot me."

Gabe slightly rearranged his expression, apparently insulted. "I wouldn't have missed. Not ever."

Leigh prayed she'd never have to test his accuracy again. "Well, thank you. That's twice you've saved my life."

"Don't thank me yet. We're not out of danger. We have to get away from here first."

Leigh silently agreed. One man was dead, but there were at least three others who would probably be willing to do what their comrade had tried.

Gabe stopped when they reached a large metal door at the end of the room and turned to her. "Here are the rules. Stay behind me at all times. I want us back to back, moving together. Got that?"

"Yes, I think so." Leigh hoped so anyway. She still felt woozy, and Gabe's quickly spoken instructions seemed jumbled.

"Rule two—you watch our backs, and I'll take care of anything that comes from any other direction." He tipped his head to her gun. "By any chance, do you remember how to use that?"

She eyed the weapon as if it was a foreign object. "Maybe."

Gabe repeated that, adding a soundless word of profanity. "All right. If you have to shoot, hold the gun level and brace your wrist with your left hand. That's a lot of firepower, and I don't want you dropping your weapon when you feel the recoil. Shoot to kill. Understand?''

Gabe didn't wait for her to answer, not that Leigh had anything to say about the abbreviated lesson on how to kill. He spun her around so they were back to back. He eased open the door and peered into the parking lot.

The alarm started almost immediately. It wasn't a typical security system that clamored loudly enough to be heard blocks away. It was a piercing hum, but it was certainly meant to serve as a warning.

''All right. Let's go,'' Gabe said. ''Remember everything I've told you.''

Leigh didn't know how he expected her to do that. She literally couldn't remember her name so how would she keep all the other things straight? Maybe she'd get lucky, and her instincts would kick in if she had to shoot.

The night air engulfed her when they stepped outside. It was humid, almost stifling. Even with the drone of the alarm, the place was eerily silent. No traffic noise. No birds. Nothing. Just the sound of their steps as Gabe orchestrated them away from the building.

*Shoot to kill,* he'd told her. That made sense because a wounded gunman could still have a deadly aim. She had to wonder if she could kill. Or if she'd ever killed before.

God, that seemed an awful thing not to know.

Gabe skirted along a row of shrubs, following the semistraight line until they came to a Dumpster. They ducked behind it just as the door to the laundry area flew open. Milky yellow light poured out into the darkness.

So did two armed men.

Gabe latched onto her hand and forced her to run. "Stay with me."

Shots shattered the near silence, sounding so close that Leigh didn't want to know just how close they were coming to Gabe and her. She lost count of how many times the guns fired, but they seemed to keep pace with her racing heartbeat.

Leigh hadn't remembered her flip-flops or her hurt ankle until they started to sprint. Not ideal running shoes, and the stitches tore at her skin. Somehow, Gabe managed to keep her on her feet, even when they left the pavement and darted over a patch of uneven ground.

The yard, such that it was, melted into a greenbelt cluttered with stubby trees and rocks. An eight-foot-high masonry fence was just beyond that. Gabe didn't ask if it was something she could climb—he just scaled it, dragging her like a rag doll with him.

When they reached the other side, she noticed the motorcycle. It was nestled between two scrub oaks, but not even the darkness could camouflage the chrome.

"We're riding that?" she asked in a frantic whisper.

"Yes." He slipped his gun back into his shoulder

holster, straddled the leather seat and started the engine. ''Keep your weapon handy. We just might need it before this is over.''

She nodded. Somewhere behind them, close behind, those men were probably gaining ground. Still, she took the time to eye the motorcycle. ''Do you have helmets?''

''No!''

It wouldn't do any good to point out that riding without helmets was dangerous. He'd no doubt point out that bullets and gunmen were even more deadly.

And he'd be right.

Gabe didn't try to alleviate her fears. He merely latched onto her wrist and hauled her on the bike behind him. Within seconds, he had the motorcycle rumbling through the night and away from the gunmen.

Leigh quickly learned she had to hang on or fall off, and the easiest thing to hang on to was Gabe. While still clinging to the gun, she wrapped her arms around his waist, pressed her cheek to his back and held on. And she prayed, hoping the God of whichever religion she professed would hear her. Right now, she needed someone of a divine nature on her side.

After all, she was with a man who killed as easily as he breathed, and Leigh knew all too well that he held her life—and possibly even her heart—in his hands.

# *Chapter Four*

Gabe had a lot of questions. And too few answers.

That did not please him.

He was reasonably sure he'd lost the hired guns. Fairly certain he could remember his way down the dirt roads that snaked around the bayou. And he was hopeful he'd managed to save their lives. For the time being anyway. However, he wasn't at all sure what the heck was going on. Or who'd just tried to kill them.

Still, none of those things occupied his thoughts for long. It was the woman behind him that he couldn't get off his mind. His wife.

At the clinic, Jinx had ordered him to be nice to Leigh. But that was only the tip of the flipping iceberg. They also wanted him to lie through his teeth. He was supposed to tell her everything was all right between them. That they'd had problems in the past but had worked them all out.

Yeah, right.

Between the lies and being nice, he was also supposed to get her to trust him. Just like that. He was supposed to erase all the bad feelings between them and regain her confidence. He'd have an easier time forgetting that she'd ever been his wife.

However, it didn't matter if the task was impossible. The Justice Department expected him to give his all. Heck, he'd already done that.

And then he'd made it worse by kissing her.

That shouldn't have happened. What the devil had he been thinking when he put his mouth on hers? That was just it—he hadn't thought. He'd acted. Reacted. And much to his disgust, he'd even enjoyed it. He couldn't let it happen again, not with so much at stake.

Easy to say. Hard to do.

It was especially hard since she was right behind him. She had her arms wrapped around his waist—apparently holding on for dear life. No surprise there. Leigh hated motorcycles.

Of course, she probably hated him, too.

He wouldn't mention that to her yet. If she was faking this amnesia, then she already knew how she felt about him. If her memory loss was real, it would be a stupid time to remind her of their past.

Gabe drove nearly two hours before he stopped. Until then, he stayed on narrow dirt roads, using only the moonlight to keep him out of the ditches. When he finally found familiar ground, he pulled the motorcycle into a clutter of trees and turned off the engine.

''Any idea where we are?'' Leigh asked, climbing

off the seat. She massaged her backside and made a few sounds of discomfort.

He got off, too, and stretched. ''Between Baton Rouge and New Orleans.'' Actually, they were still very close to New Orleans, but he'd taken the most circuitous route to get there. Hopefully, that had given Jinx enough time to get a few things under control. If not, then it would be one long night.

''Are we safe here?''

Gabe glanced around at the dense brush. ''Hopefully.''

''You don't sound hopeful.''

He shrugged. ''Guarantees are a rare thing in life, Leigh, but we're a heck of lot safer here than we were back at that clinic.''

She stayed quiet a moment. ''And you don't believe those men will follow us here?''

''No.'' Well, he was almost certain they wouldn't anyway. Getting to this particular area of the bayou wasn't easy unless a person knew the way. He knew the way. God willing, the gunmen didn't.

''So, is this the part when you tell me what's really going on?'' she asked.

Gabe groaned. He didn't want to play a question-and-answer game tonight. *Keep her alive. Catch the bad guys.* Oh yeah, and, *Be nice to her.* At no time had anyone said a thing about answering her questions.

''You know what's going on,'' Gabe briskly assured her. "Some gunmen came after us, and we got away."

"There's more to it than that. How about letting me in on who those men are and why they want to kill us?"

"That, *mi vida,* is the big question of the day."

"Are you saying you don't know who's behind this?" She didn't wait for him to confirm that. "That breach of security at the clinic didn't happen by itself. And who's to blame for that, huh? Who was in charge of guarding the place?"

Gabe spat out some profanity. "The FBI."

Her mouth dropped open. "Your own people? Well, that's just great."

It didn't exactly please Gabe either, but the breach hadn't necessarily come from anyone in the Bureau, especially not from Jinx. It could have been an outside source. In other words, he still had nothing definite. Gabe didn't like that. He wanted something *definite.*

"Come on," he insisted. "We need to get moving."

"On foot?"

"Well, since there's deep mud ahead, and the motorcycle would get stuck, I don't see any other way." And with that, he took her gun, put it in the waist of his jeans and snagged her around the hips. Like a caveman claiming his woman, he tossed her over his shoulder.

"Hey! What the devil do you think you're doing?" Leigh complained.

Gabe began to walk, keeping the same pace he would have had she not been on his shoulder. "Carrying you."

She wiggled, squirmed and otherwise tried to twist her way out of his grip. "Put me down!"

"No can do. You have stitches in your ankle, remember? Now, let's see if I can recall basic first aid." He pretended to think about it. "By now, those stitches have probably worked their way partially loose, so you have an open wound. Add to that some of this sloppy, wormy mud, and I see the potential for a really nasty infection. What do you think?" He didn't let her answer. "I don't have time to take you to the doctor, so be still."

Just like that, Leigh stopped struggling, and her body practically went limp against him. "I suppose it's too much to hope that other than traipsing through a swamp, you actually have a plan?"

He made his way around a large cypress tree and its kneelike roots that stood almost a foot above the ground. "I have one, but I don't feel especially good about it."

*Keep her alive. Catch the bad guys.* Nope, he didn't feel good about that plan at all. It definitely lacked the necessary components for a successful mission.

"It'd be a heck of a lot easier if you just had your memory," Gabe let her know. "Are you sure you're not faking this amnesia?"

"No, I'm not faking it. You've already asked me that. Besides, why would I fake something like this?"

He could think of a reason. Leigh could be using the ploy so she wouldn't have to tell him why she'd really returned. "I don't have an answer to that one either, *mi vida.*"

She poked him hard on the back. "Don't call me darling."

Gabe grinned in spite of his rotten mood. Well, she remembered some of her Spanish anyway, along with remembering that she didn't like him to use that little term of endearment. And that's why he'd done it. Maybe he could work it into the conversation again. Numerous times. It might make him feel better if she was as annoyed as he was.

He stopped on a solid patch of ground, deposited Leigh on her feet and pulled back some low branches. Just as he hoped it would be, there was the truck hidden behind the curtain of Spanish moss.

"Thank you, Jinx," Gabe mumbled and opened the door on the driver's side. "I owe you another one."

"Jinx?" she asked. "What does he have to do with this?"

"He left this truck here for us, and he sent that warning over the pager to tell us those gunmen were in the parking lot." Gabe pulled down some moss and used it to clean the mud off his boots. "We'll spend the night here and head out at first light."

Leigh stared at him. "Here?"

"Yes, *here.*" Gabe motioned for her to get inside. He slapped at a couple of mosquitoes that started to feast on his neck. "And hurry up before these things eat us alive."

She got in all right, after a loud huff, and she scooted toward the other side to get as far away from him as possible. Even then, they were practically shoulder to shoulder when Gabe joined her.

"Might as well get comfortable," he told her.

Her eyebrow arched. "You're kidding, right?"

Yeah. He was. There wasn't much chance of getting comfortable on a narrow seat with Leigh. Still, it probably wasn't a good idea to say that to her. It would only start another round of questions.

He pulled off his T-shirt and tossed it on the floor along with his holster and all three weapons. "We'll have to leave the windows up because of the mosquitoes, so it'll get hot in here. Wanna take off those scrubs?"

She gave him a look that could have withered a new fence post. "Not even if I were on fire and there wasn't a drop of water for miles around."

He chuckled and draped his forearm over the steering wheel. "Lie down."

She glanced at the seat. And then at his bare chest. "You want me to lie down?"

He rolled his eyes. "Hell. Leigh, we're married. And even if we weren't, we'd still have to get some rest. That means the seat or outside. I have no intentions of sleeping outside with the snakes and mosquitoes, do you?"

She looked out the window, apparently to weigh her

options. Not that she had any options to weigh. She must have figured that out because without a sound, she lay on the seat. With her feet only inches from him, she let her hand dangle over the guns.

Gabe spun her around like a top and put her head right next to his lap.

With her eyes narrowed to slits, Leigh stared up at him. "Is there any particular reason you're treating me like a prisoner?"

"You bet. I know you too well. Right now, you figure you can't trust anyone but yourself. You wonder whose side I'm on. In the next hour or so, you'll start to think you need to get away from me, even at the risk of becoming gator bait. Well, until you figure out I'm the best thing you've got going, then I'm staying close. Understand?"

Her mouth twisted as if she'd tasted something sour. "Yes, I understand." She rolled onto her side, facing the back of the seat. Immediately, she made a strange sound.

"Now what?" he snarled.

"The seat smells like fishing bait."

Unfortunately, she didn't smell like bait, but it might have been better for him if she had. Since she was so close, Gabe couldn't avoid taking in her scent. The smell of the scrubs. Mixed with that was the hint of warm leather from the motorcycle seat. There was sweat, not stale and heavy, but just a hint. And beneath all of that was Leigh's own unique scent. Distinctively female.

And more than a little distracting.

It was a challenge, but Gabe had to prevent that scent from turning his brain to mush. He forced himself to remember what she'd done. It worked. Until she spoke.

"We don't get along very well, do we, Sanchez?"

He considered lying. A Justice Department slant on the truth. But there was something in her voice. A plea for the truth, and the truth was exactly what he gave her. "No. We don't."

She paused, apparently letting that sink in. "If our situations were reversed, would you trust me?"

Now he'd lie. Except it wouldn't really be a lie. Yes, their past had been, well, checkered. But if it were a matter of life or death, Leigh would come through for him. Gabe didn't have to guess about that.

"I'd trust you," he finally said. "Now, give it a rest and go to—"

"I hate being like this."

"Sorry, but it's the best I can offer under the circumstances. I promise, there was a time when you didn't mind sleeping this close to me."

"I'm not talking about that. Not entirely anyway," she added apparently as an afterthought. "I hate not knowing who I am or who you are. You could be an ax murderer, and I wouldn't know until it was too late."

She looked up at him. Gabe looked down and met her gaze in the moonlight. He didn't want to stare at her, but his body seemed to have a different idea. It was hard not to remember that this was a woman he'd once loved. A woman who'd loved him right back. Then, things had fallen apart.

And that was a whole set of memories he didn't want to deal with right now.

"I'm not an ax murderer," he heard himself say. "I gave that up years ago."

She actually smiled, briefly, but there was a frown not too far behind. "I know nothing about you or me except the few things you've let me know. I don't even know my middle name. I'm too scared to admit I'm scared because I don't know if I can trust you with that admission of weakness. I'm afraid you'll use it against me."

"Leigh." His voice was gruff. Then it changed. It softened. His hand was already on her hair. It was definitely intimate contact, but he didn't pull away. Gabe figured he would kick himself for it later. "Being scared doesn't mean you're weak. It just means you're scared. And smart. Stupid people are too stupid to be scared. By the way, your middle name is Ann."

"Ann," she repeated on a heavy sigh. "It doesn't even sound familiar."

Gabe said nothing. He leaned his head against the cool window and listened to the sound of her voice.

"I don't know what I was. Who I am. You don't know how frustrating that is."

Oh yes he did. Gabe knew a lot about frustration. After all, Leigh was right next to him, and more than anything, he wanted to touch her. Maybe even kiss her again. The old wounds stopped him. And the fact she'd probably slap him if he tried to do anything like that. She didn't know about the old wounds, but that didn't mean she trusted him.

"I seem to know a little bit about a lot of things," she continued. "Like I knew the clinical name for my amnesia, but I didn't know you. What was I, Gabe? And don't you dare say I worked in a bookstore in Austin, because I know that's not right."

He debated telling her since the truth would just create more questions. But without the truth, he didn't stand of chance of tapping into her mind to find out what had gone wrong.

"You were an FBI agent," Gabe answered. "The last year you were with the Bureau, you were part of the ERT, the Evidence Response Team."

"Yes." She nodded. Paused. And repeated it. "Now, that feels right."

It should. She'd been one of the best. "You resigned after all of this happened with the corrupt government official."

She pushed out a deep breath. Of relief, maybe. It didn't feel much like relief to Gabe. Her warm breath dusted his bare stomach. Not good. Maybe he should have risked roasting and kept his shirt on after all.

He inched slightly away from her. Not that he could *inch* very far without leaving the truck.

"So, I was working for the FBI and came across evidence against this official? Then what happened?" she asked.

"Things resolved themselves. At least we thought they had." He shrugged. "And then you disappeared."

Leigh started to come off the seat, but Gabe laid a hand on her shoulder to stop her. That would put her mouth much to close to his. He couldn't handle that right now. Best to keep as much distance between their mouths as possible. Another of those husbandly kisses was the last thing either of them needed.

"I think you left because of me," Gabe said, anticipating her next question. "We'd talked about a divorce." It was the truth, even though it was something Jinx and Walters had ordered him not to tell her. "It's late. We should get some—"

"You didn't know where I was all this time?"

Hell, she just didn't intend to stop. "Sometimes I knew," he admitted. "But I couldn't quite catch up with you."

"Was I ever in Houston?"

"Probably." And he made a mental note that it was the second time she'd mentioned that particular city. "You're originally from Dallas. Why? Do you remember something about Houston?"

"Not really. It's just a place that keeps coming to mind, but I can't associate it with anything. Houston might mean nothing." A moment later, she dismissed it with a wave of her hand. "I have to ask. Considering our marital problems, just how hard did you look for me during the past two years?"

"I looked," he said defensively. "You're the one

who walked out. You didn't want anyone to find you.''

''Apparently someone found me,'' she pointed out.

''Maybe. Or maybe you had no choice but to be found. Sometimes things play out that way.''

She stared up at him. ''What does that mean?''

''It means you need to get some sleep.'' Gabe yawned. Not a fake one either. It'd been a hell of a long day, and he was bone-tired. ''Who knows? You might wake up tomorrow and remember everything.''

She didn't disagree, but the little sound she made wasn't one of hope. Still, at the moment, hope was about the best thing they had going for them.

Hope that Leigh would regain her memory.

Hope that those gunmen would stop following them.

Hope that he could, somehow, keep her alive.

# Chapter Five

Leigh awakened slowly, trying to get her bearings before she moved or even opened her eyes. Her bearings, however, were wrapped all around her. She was on the truck seat cradled in a man's arms. Gabe's arms. Her face was buried against his neck, and his musky scent surrounded her.

This was not good. Not good at all. That scent went straight through her like a triple shot of whiskey. Not a memory, exactly. More like a feeling that what they were doing was right.

And wrong.

Quickly but not so easily, she unraveled herself from his snug grip so she could get to a sitting position. The moment she moved, Gabe did as well. He came off the seat, reaching for his gun in the same motion.

Their gazes collided. His eyes were still ripe with sleep, and she saw some of the emotions that he'd kept so guarded, so under control the day before. The concern. The stress.

And other things she didn't even want to explore.

Leigh took a deep breath. Just who was this man that she'd once promised to love forever? She was almost afraid to find out.

Pulling herself away from that naked gaze, and from his partly naked body, Leigh opened the truck door and stepped out, careful not to put direct pressure on her wounded ankle. She made a sweeping glance around the thick cypress woods. The sun was just rising over a misty-topped bayou, and with the exception of a snow-white egret, they were alone.

Completely alone.

"Are you all right?" Gabe asked.

No, she wasn't. Reality was even harsher in the early-morning light than it had been in the darkness. She was in the middle of a bayou with a man she didn't know. She had no memory. And someone wanted her dead. Not the best way to start the day. Oh, and she was scared. Add to that a wicked headache and what felt like an overwhelming need for a cup of coffee, and it didn't seem she had a lot to look forward to.

Leigh leaned against the truck and tried to catch her breath. "So, what happens now?" she asked, almost afraid to hear the answer.

With catlike grace, Gabe slid off the seat and stood beside her. He brought his shoulder holster and gun with him, draping it over his arm. "We try to find out who's behind this and then get you to a safer place."

At least he seemed to think that was possible. She

wasn't so sure anymore. Maybe there were no safe places to go.

She glanced at him out of the corner of her eye. Still shirtless, the sunlight danced over his deeply tanned chest. And the jeans. God, the jeans. They gloved parts of him that she wished weren't so gloved.

Those were things she definitely shouldn't notice.

Still, it was hard not to notice and respond to him since he was an attractive man. Even if they hadn't shared a past she couldn't remember, that attraction probably would have still been there.

The attraction.

The emotions.

The uncertainty of their past.

Those things frightened Leigh almost as much as coming face-to-face with the person who'd tried to kill her. Eventually, she would have to remember what had torn Gabe and her apart. Leigh wasn't exactly looking forward to reliving any of that.

Gabe lifted the lid on the storage bin in the bed of the truck. Muscles flexed as he fished around inside and came up with two bottles of water. ''I don't guess your memory returned overnight, huh?'' He passed one of the bottles her way.

Leigh shook her head. No memory. Just a headache and an unwanted physical attraction to the man who leaned against the truck beside her.

She didn't plan to ask him to put on his shirt. No sense letting him in on the fact there was a whirl of emotions she didn't understand, or want to feel. Emotions that included a good old-fashioned case of lust. She might not remember Gabe, but her hormones sure did.

He took a long drink of water. "So, nothing about this place seems familiar?"

Leigh looked around again, hoping she'd missed something that would jar her memory. She hadn't. "No, should it?"

Gabe shrugged. "We spent our honeymoon not too far from here."

"We had our honeymoon in the middle of a bayou?" she asked, sure that she'd heard him wrong. It didn't seem the best of locations for that. Or maybe it did. If two people wanted complete privacy, it would be ideal.

Leigh quickly shoved that thought aside.

"We were in a cabin just a couple of miles away," Gabe added. "We didn't go there last night because it's a little too close to the main road." He stared out at the scenery, and Leigh could almost see the memories going through his head. Memories no doubt of all the things that couples did on a honeymoon.

Oh. Mercy.

It didn't seem a subject she should press, but it was also one she couldn't resist. After all, she'd spent two years with this man. "We were in love?"

She saw the muscles stiffen in Gabe's arms and shoulders. He put the bottle to his mouth, finished off the water and tossed the plastic container in the back of the truck. "Yeah. Once."

His answer wasn't just brusque. It was downright chilly. And that chill made Leigh want to know more. However, she didn't get a chance to delve any deeper into the feelings they'd once had for each other. The slight sound she heard caused her throat to snap shut.

Gabe obviously heard something too because without warning he caught onto her arm and shoved her to the ground. Suddenly, her face, and the rest of her, was in the moist dirt. He followed on top on her, sprawling himself over her back.

Pebbles and other assorted debris dug into her stomach and chest. Other than an involuntary groan caused by the weight of Gabe's body on hers, Leigh didn't even have time to react. She heard the gunmetal whisper against the stiff leather holster as Gabe drew his weapon.

All her fears returned in full force. Her heart started to pound. Her stomach twisted into a hard knot. God, she didn't want to die, and there might be nothing she could do to stop it. She couldn't even reach for her gun since it was inside the truck.

Leigh tried to look around, to see if there was any real danger. Maybe it was nothing at all—a sound made by some bayou animal or the morning breeze rustling through the trees. But she was almost positive an animal hadn't made that sound.

"I'd appreciate it a whole lot if you didn't shoot me," the man called out. "This shirt is new, and I don't want blood all over it."

With that calmly delivered, satirical remark, she felt

Gabe relax. "It's all right," he assured her. "It's just Jinx."

*Jinx.* That didn't make her breathe any easier. Gabe seemed to trust the man, but Leigh wasn't about to dismiss that prickle that crawled up the back of her neck. After all, that breach in security at the clinic had happened on Jinx's watch.

Gabe lifted himself off her. Not easily. And not before his hand grazed the side of her right breast. Leigh pretended not to notice, but pretending didn't do a thing to stop her breath from shuddering. If Gabe noticed, he didn't say anything. Which was just as well. Instead, he caught onto her hand and helped her to her feet.

"What's he doing out here?" she asked none too pleasantly.

"He owns this place. And the cabin where we stayed on our honeymoon."

Leigh didn't have time to react to that, but she intended to give it some thought later.

"Gabe. Leigh," Jinx greeted, making his way through the ferns and jewelweed toward them. He stopped only inches away and pointed to the path that Leigh had already noticed. "I parked up there. No one followed me, but I covered my tracks just in case. By the way, glad you two made it out of that clinic."

"It took some doing." Gabe reholstered his gun. "Thanks for the heads up."

"No problem." Jinx's gaze raked over her. "So, did you get your memory back?"

"No."

Jinx didn't respond to that. He simply handed Gabe a plain black gym bag and a small cooler. "That means she can't help us with that little problem we discussed."

"What little problem?" Leigh asked.

"We were hoping you'd be able to tell us who tried to kill you," Gabe insisted.

As critical as that sounded, she was sure there was still a heck of a lot more to it than that. She doubted it was a coincidence that Jinx's comment had been vague.

Gabe set the cooler in the truck and handed the gym bag to her. "There should be some clothes in here so you can change. Those hospital scrubs are too noticeable."

He was right, of course, especially since the top had spatters of blood on it. Still, she didn't think it was a change of attire that Gabe had on his mind. It seemed he was rather anxious for her to leave so he could talk privately with his friend.

Leigh accommodated him. Well, in a way. She stepped behind a large bell-bottom tree about fifteen feet away, but she kept her ear turned toward the men. Unfortunately, the breeze didn't cooperate, and she could only catch snatches of what they said. She heard something about Agent Teresa Walters wanting them to "come in immediately."

Without taking her attention away from the conversation, she went through the bag and found a phone, ammunition and a first-aid kit. There was also an envelope stuffed with cash. The only clothes were a pair of very short shorts and a cotton top. No shoes, which meant she'd have to wear the flip-flops a while longer.

Leigh snatched up the phone and turned it on. She'd hoped she would dial something automatically—a number so rote, so ingrained, that it would come to her in spite of the amnesia. That didn't happen.

Nothing happened.

Apparently, there was no critical phone number lurking in her memory. It was another dead end. That meant she'd have to try to get something out of Gabe and Jinx.

Not good.

She hadn't had a lot of success in that particular area. So far, all she knew was two years earlier she'd uncovered something dirty about a man named Joe Dayton. Now someone wanted her dead because of that.

Well, maybe.

And maybe it had nothing to do with Joe Dayton at all. Maybe something else had triggered these attacks. Of course, Leigh had no way of knowing because everything was still trapped inside her head.

Frustrated, she tossed the phone back into the bag and peeled off the scrubs so she could change into the other clothes.

"Philip," she heard Gabe say, making the name sound like profanity.

"You think Leigh will know where he is?" Jinx

added another question to that, but Leigh couldn't catch what he said.

"Maybe. She mentioned Houston in the message she left on my machine."

Leigh heard that part. Clearly. And again she felt that tug of familiarity. She didn't know anything about that message she'd left Gabe, but getting to Houston was important. Critical even. Too bad she didn't know why. Maybe it had something to do with this man named Philip.

So, who was this guy—a boyfriend? But that didn't feel right.

She bent down to pick up the shorts. And then she saw it. Or rather saw *them.* "Oh my God," she whispered.

Three thin, vertical scars were on her stomach, just above the top of her panties. The whitish lines were so faint, so threadlike, that she figured that's why she hadn't noticed them when she was in the bathroom at the clinic.

They looked like stretch marks.

That possibility caused her to reach for the tree for support. Stretch marks. God, had she been pregnant? Maybe. Leigh carried that out to its next logical conclusion—had she had a child?

Certainly Gabe would have mentioned something as monumental as that. Wouldn't he? Leigh gave it more thought. Yes, he would have. There would have been no reason to keep something like that from her.

Well, unless he didn't know.

But that didn't make sense either. Like the scar on her arm, these didn't look fresh. Besides, a woman could get stretch marks for a variety of reasons—weight gain or just plain genetics. Those explanations were far easier to accept than the possibility that she had a child out there somewhere.

Far easier.

"Everything all right?" Gabe called out to her.

No, it wasn't, but Leigh didn't say that to him. "I'm almost done."

And the first chance she got, she intended to ask Gabe a few questions.

She pulled on the shorts, frowning at the fact that they fit like skin. There wasn't much of the waist-length top either, but since she didn't have a choice, she slipped it on anyway.

The men were still speaking in whispers when she came out from behind the tree. "I'm ready," she let Gabe know.

He was in midsentence, still speaking to Jinx, but the words seemed to freeze in his throat. Surprise rifled through his eyes. Then something else. Something smoldering, no doubt caused by the skimpy clothes. Gabe slid that smoldering gaze from her head to her toes, and that gaze did more than concern Leigh. It heated every drop of blood in her body.

"What's the plan?" she asked no one in particular. Best to move on from smoldering looks to business.

Gabe cleared his throat and motioned toward the truck. "We put some distance between us and New

Orleans. I need to get you to a safe place so we can start making a few inquiries.''

That certainly sounded like a good idea. And while they were putting that distance between them and New Orleans, she would see what she could learn from Gabe. ''Are we going to Houston?''

Gabe glanced at Jinx first. ''Maybe. Eventually.''

''What's in Houston, Leigh?'' Jinx questioned. But it was more than a question. It was a challenge.

She shrugged. ''You tell me. According to you, I'm just a bookstore employee.''

The corner of Gabe's mouth lifted, but he quickly covered it with his hand.

There seemed to be some amusement on Jinx's face as well, but it didn't make it to his voice. ''I don't think it's my imagination that you don't trust me.'' He didn't wait for her to confirm that. ''Would it help if you knew I was Gabe's best man at your wedding?''

Leigh glanced at Gabe, and he verified that information with a nod. However, it didn't do a thing to change her opinion of Jinx. There was something about him, something she couldn't quite put her finger on. Something that caused that prickle to return to her neck. Still, it was best not to antagonize him.

''You and I want the same thing,'' she finally said. ''I want to find out who's after me, and I want to try to figure out who I am. I'm hoping Gabe can fill me in on some more of the details.''

It was subtle, but because Leigh kept her focus on Jinx, she saw him slip Gabe a warning glance. So, there were other things that Jinx didn't want her to know. Maybe those things involved the stretch marks that she just couldn't get off her mind, or maybe it involved the man named Philip. Perhaps Philip was the key to finding out what was going on.

Gabe opened the truck door and motioned for her to get in. "It's time to go."

Leigh was more than ready to leave, especially since she was sure Jinx wouldn't be going with them. She climbed onto the seat, and Gabe shut the door. He whispered something to Jinx before he joined her.

"Be careful," Jinx said to them as Gabe started the engine. "And if I were you, I wouldn't trust anybody until we have some answers."

Jinx obviously didn't include himself in that blanket warning, but Leigh silently added him to it. It was excellent advice, and she intended to take it. She didn't intend to trust anyone.

# *Chapter Six*

"I have a question," Leigh announced. She drank some water and settled against the seat as if this would be a long-drawn-out ordeal.

Gabe figured it likely would be in just about every way possible.

"Just one question?" he asked.

"Well, actually, I have several, but I guess this is as good a place to start as any. Do we have a child?"

Gabe felt as if a bolt of lightning had hit him. He was almost afraid to find out what had prompted that question. "No," he quickly assured her.

"You're sure?"

He didn't even have to think about his answer. "Positive. Why'd you ask?"

She shrugged. "No reason. I just figured since we, uh, were married, there was a possibility we had a child."

"No. We'd decided not to have children."

He braced himself for yet more on the subject, but Leigh stayed quiet for several moments. Hell. What was going on in her head? Did she remember something, and if so, why had she remembered that particular piece of their past? That one issue had been the source of too many arguments to count.

"So, no baby," she mumbled under her breath. "Did I used to weigh more than I do now?"

Gabe glanced at her. "A little. What the heck is this all about, Leigh?" With everything else going on, he couldn't imagine that she'd be concerned about her weight.

She shrugged again. "I just got the feeling that I'm thinner than I usually am. I guess maybe a ton of stress is the ultimate diet, huh?"

Gabe thought maybe that was a smoke screen, but he didn't care. He was more than happy to let the subject drop. It wasn't a good idea for them to discuss anything about her body. It would only remind him that she had a body. A body that he was familiar with in every intimate kind of way.

"Okay. Here's something else I'd like to know," she continued a moment later. "Who's Philip?"

Gabe blew out a frustrated breath. Even though he'd known more questions would be coming, he didn't need this any more than a possible baby/weight-loss discussion. The traffic on the highway was light, but he wanted to keep his attention focused on their surroundings. That wouldn't be easy to do if he had to answer a lot of questions. Her clothes already gave him more distractions than he needed. Jinx was obviously trying to torture him.

The first problem was her shorts. They were snug in all the wrong places and showed practically every inch of her long, slender legs. The top wasn't much better, especially since she obviously wasn't wearing a bra. Gabe saw the outline of her nipples. Hard to concentrate on anything else when his mind kept going back to those.

However, Gabe forced his attention back on the immediate problem—Leigh's question. A question that he knew would just lead to others. "Let me guess. You eavesdropped on my conversation with Jinx?"

"I *overheard,*" she corrected. "So who is this Philip? Is he the person who tried to kill me?"

Hell, he hoped not, but Gabe was almost positive Philip had no part in this. That didn't mean the man didn't have information, and with some luck, Jinx might soon know where they could find him so they could get that information. "No, he's your brother."

That improved her posture. Leigh barely got down the mouthful of water she'd just drunk. She obviously hadn't considered the possibility that she had family.

"I have a brother," she mumbled under her breath. "What about him and my parents? Certainly they're worried about me. I hadn't considered that someone might be concerned as to my whereabouts."

Oh, he was pretty sure there were plenty of people concerned. The right people. And the wrong ones. The problem was determining which category everyone belonged in.

"Your father died about ten years ago when you

were in your first year of college,'' Gabe explained. ''Your mother remarried some guy from England, and you haven't spoken to her in ages. But you and Philip—that's a different story. He's your only sibling, and I'm sure you've kept in touch with him. Too bad we don't know where he is.''

''Yes, too bad.''

She leaned closer. Too close. From that angle Gabe could see right down that skimpy top. He quickly turned away, but that one glance made his body clench. And beg. Gabe decided it was a great time to keep his eyes straight ahead.

''When we were still at the clinic and that man had a gun on me, you said that I had money,'' Leigh commented. ''Any truth to that?''

''All truth. You're loaded. Your father invented some little gadget on an offshore oil rig. When he died, he left just about everything to you and Philip. Of course, Philip blew most of his on expensive wine, cheap women and there's-a-sucker-born-every-minute business ventures. When his inheritance was gone, he managed to talk you out of some of yours, but you still have plenty.''

''So, I'm not broke. That's good.''

It wasn't something he'd ever expected Leigh to say. She'd always dismissed her sizable inheritance, rarely tapping into it except for emergencies. But Gabe had to remind himself, again, that the woman sitting next to him wasn't Leigh. Not the old Leigh anyway. Even if she hadn't had amnesia, the past two years would have probably changed her in many ways. It had certainly changed him.

"Is having money important to you?" he asked.

She nodded. "It is if I need long-term medical care to help restore my memory."

So, that's all there was to it. Gabe didn't know why that made him feel better. Nothing about their situation—except for the fact they were alive—should make him feel better.

Especially that outfit she wore.

Gabe took a deep breath and forced his attention back on the conversation. "I suspect if you hadn't had such unlimited funds, I'd have found you sooner."

"Maybe," she agreed. "If I have so much money, why was I working at that bookstore in Austin?"

Gabe smiled. The woman didn't miss a thing. "I believe you wanted to make us think you were working there. Jinx and I spent some off-duty time staking it out, but I never saw you in the place."

"Ah, I get the truth, finally." With that look of triumph on her face, she pressed her foot to the dash.

That wasn't the best place she could have put her foot. Nope. It caused the shorts to ride up even higher, and Gabe got more than an eyeful of her thigh. This might be his estranged wife, and a woman who didn't remember him, but his body had no trouble recalling why he'd been attracted to her in the first place.

"That's a good start," she continued. She was obviously unaware of the effect she had on him. If she glanced in the direction of his jeans, however, she just might see that effect. "But rather than me ask a whole bunch of question that you might or might not answer, why don't you tell me what's really going on?"

That encompassed a whole lot of territory. Territory that Jinx and Teresa didn't want him to cover, but Gabe wasn't so sure there was any reason to keep things from Leigh. After all, it was a long drive to the safe house, and recounting her life history might jog her memory. It would no doubt jog his as well, but Gabe figured he didn't have a choice but to relive some of the things—both good and bad—that had gone on between them.

Besides, he needed something to get his mind off those clothes.

"Well?" Leigh prompted.

Gabe didn't pull any punches. "About eight months ago, I stepped up my search to find you when I learned someone was going through the Justice Department's computer files to try to locate you."

Because she was so close to him, he heard her breath hitch. "Who was doing that?"

"I don't know. But it's not just a hacker, nor is it someone who's idly curious. These probes are specific, calculated and thorough. And they specifically lead to you. Or at least that's what they're trying to lead to. I don't think the person was any more successful than Jinx and I were, but they've been at it a lot longer than we have. In fact, this person has apparently been searching for you since you disappeared two years ago."

Her tone took on a new urgency. "They've used my name in these probes?"

"Yes, and your brother's."

"My God." Leigh touched her fingertips to her mouth. "This person that's trying to kill me might go after my brother, too?"

Hell. Just about all the color drained from her face. That was something he probably should have waited to tell her.

Gabe resisted the urge to reach out and comfort her. But it wasn't easy. *Keep her alive. Catch the bad guys. Be nice to her.* Getting involved with her again wasn't on that list, and he wasn't about to add it either.

There wasn't much he could do about the physical attraction his body still had for her, but there was a hell of a lot he could do to stop himself from getting emotionally involved with her again.

"I don't think anyone's after Philip," he let her know. Gabe gripped the steering wheel to make sure he didn't slide his hand in her direction. If he wasn't careful, he might take that *be nice to her* and turn it into an excuse to hold her hand. "I think they just wanted to use him to try to locate you."

"Maybe they were successful," she said softly.

Yes. And that was all the more reason to find Philip, so Gabe could make sure he was safe and stayed that way. "I think what's going on has to do with Joe Dayton, the corrupt Justice Department official that we talked about last night."

"The one you don't want to tell me much about."

It was on the tip of Gabe's tongue to deny that, but then he realized it was true. He didn't want to talk about Dayton nor about what had gone on right before Leigh left him.

Too bad it was necessary.

So, just how should he go about delivering what might be a bombshell? If she'd turned ashy at the mention that her brother might be in danger, what he was about to tell her certainly wasn't going to do anything to calm her fears. Still, it was vital information that she eventually had to know.

"Two years ago you came across some information that led you to Dayton," Gabe explained, trying to sound clinical. He'd just give her the bare facts and then hope like the devil it jogged something in her memory. "He was involved in a plot to sell huge quantities of weapons—items that the Justice Department had originally confiscated in various raids throughout the country."

"I see," Leigh said after several moments. "And Dayton's after me because I learned this information?"

"No. Dayton's out of the picture. He committed suicide a couple of days after you found the evidence. Unfortunately, he killed himself before we could learn where he'd stored all those weapons."

She didn't say anything. She sat there apparently processing that information.

"The one behind all of this is more than likely Dayton's accomplice," Gabe continued. He made the turn that would take them to the westbound highway and checked the rearview mirror to make sure no one was following them. "We never did find out who that person was. In fact, we didn't even know for certain that there was an accomplice. Not until some of those previously confiscated weapons showed up during an ATF raid of a militia compound about two weeks ago."

"You're sure the weapons were from Dayton's original cache?" she asked.

"We're sure. The weapons aren't of the ordinary variety, so we know what's out there. I'm talking some with biological and chemical components. Some are prototypes for weapons the FBI definitely doesn't want to see on the street. They're worth millions on the black market, and they're not easily moved because of the volume. My guess is they're still in the same storage facility where Joe Dayton originally had them placed."

She groaned softly, apparently grasping the motive of the person who wanted her dead.

"There's more," Gabe continued. "Those computer inquiries about you—they stopped a little over two weeks ago, at the same time those confiscated weapons showed up at the militia compound."

"I see." Yeah, she probably did. "So, the inquiries stopped because the person either found me, or he no longer needed to find me."

That's the way Gabe saw it, too, or maybe it was a combination of both. All he knew is someone wanted

Leigh dead, and it was probably all related to the person making those inquiries.

"Is it possible that I know who Dayton's accomplice is?" she asked a moment later.

"I doubt it. If you knew that person's identity, you would have gotten it to me somehow." That was a stretch of the truth. Gabe hoped she would tell him, but he had no way of knowing that for sure. However, he was sure that Leigh wouldn't have kept that kind of information to herself. Despite their personal differences, she was a law-abiding citizen.

"Unless I was trying to protect someone," Leigh added softly.

Even though she had practically whispered it, Gabe didn't miss a word. "Why would you say that?"

"I don't know." She shook her head. "I'm not sure why that came to my mind. I certainly don't remember anyone that I'd go to such lengths to protect."

She might go to such lengths to protect her brother. But that didn't make sense either because Philip had no association with Dayton. At least, Gabe was almost certain that Philip didn't, and Gabe had been looking for that connection, any connection, for two years.

"So, we're right back where we started—again." Leigh put the bottle of water she'd been drinking from back in the cooler and rested her head against the seat. "Joe Dayton's dead, and I don't know who his accomplice is."

"But that person might *think* you know something."

Just as quickly, she lifted her head. "Yes. Kill the messenger, and he'll kill the message."

"Something like that." Even though Gabe didn't like her choice of words. "Except there's another messenger."

Leigh turned to him. "What do you mean?"

"There was someone else, someone who was with you when you learned about Dayton's operation. During your search of an unrelated crime scene, you ran across a disk that detailed the proposed deal. The disk had a program virus that our systems didn't detect in time. The virus erased the data after it had been on the screen only a few minutes. You were only able to learn that the weapons were somewhere in Texas."

"That covers a lot of territory," she mumbled.

Loads. "Of course, you had no idea how important the information would be, or you would have tried other measures to remove the virus before you loaded the disk. You and a lab assistant, Frank Templeton, saw the information. No one else even got a chance to look at it."

She nodded and took it to the next logical conclusion. "Then what happened to Frank?"

"He disappeared about the same time that you did." And that might be the reason he's still alive. For that matter, he could say the same thing about Leigh.

"So Frank and I must have thought it was very important to keep our whereabouts a secret from everyone," she continued. "Including you." She angled her eyes in his direction. ‘‘Why would I do that, Gabe?’’

His stomach didn’t appreciate the question. It began to churn, and he could almost feel his blood pressure rising. It was one of the questions he would have liked to avoid, but avoiding it wouldn’t make it go away. Still, if he told her everything, she just might jump out of the truck. She most certainly wouldn’t cooperate with him.

‘‘Joe Dayton was a friend of mine, and I didn’t think he was guilty.’’ There. That was it in a nutshell. Well, a sanitized version of a nutshell anyway. ‘‘That caused some problems for us.’’

She didn’t say a word. She didn’t have to. Leigh might have had amnesia, but he recognized that look in her eyes. She was trying to piece all of this together. Eventually, she would, with or without his help.

‘‘And that’s why you and I went our separate ways?’’ she asked.

He confirmed it with a nod, but that was all he intended to confirm about their breakup. Besides, there were other things about this that she needed to know. ‘‘For two years a lot of people have been trying to track you down and find out if Frank is still alive. We needed to know what else, if anything, you two learned from that disk.’’

‘‘Well, obviously it was something that signed our death warrants. But I can’t remember a thing, so you’re back to square one.’’

‘‘Not quite,’’ Gabe explained. He checked the rearview mirror and frowned. ‘‘Frank Templeton surfaced yesterday. Just as I was leaving my apartment to meet you at the lake, he called. He said he was coming in, that he needed protection and he wanted me to provide it.’’

‘‘I take it that this isn’t a coincidence—that Frank and I came out of hiding at the same time?’’

‘‘I don’t believe in coincidences,’’ Gabe said, looking away from her. He sped up so he could pass a big-rig truck. ‘‘Something made both of you come from underground. About the time I was fishing you out of that lake, he called back and left a message on my answering machine. He wants me to meet him tomorrow night at a safe house in Grand Valley, Texas. It’s not too far from Beaumont.’’

‘‘We’re going to Grand Valley?’’

‘‘That’s the plan.’’ Gabe added some pressure to the accelerator and went around two cars. He didn’t take his attention off the rearview mirror. ‘‘Frank Templeton doesn’t have amnesia, Leigh. If anyone can give us answers…hell.’’

‘‘What’s wrong?’’

‘‘Someone’s following us.’’

# *Chapter Seven*

Leigh's gaze shot to the rearview mirror. There was a dark blue car about thirty yards behind them. Just the sight of it sent the pulse in her throat hammering. God, had those gunmen from the clinic somehow managed to find them?

"How long have they been following us?" she asked. Leigh grabbed her gun from beneath the seat and braced herself for whatever was about to happen.

"About five minutes."

That was about how long it'd been since they got on this particular highway. Despite the rush of adrenaline that raced through her body, Leigh tried to force herself to concentrate. How could those gunmen have found them so quickly? She didn't care much for any of the answers that came to mind.

"Someone tipped them off?" she suggested.

Gabe didn't answer her. He gunned the engine, passing two other vehicles. The moment he got around them, he veered off onto the next exit. The truck wobbled and shook when Gabe forced it around the tight turn.

Leigh's grip tightened on her weapon while she watched and waited to see what the other car would do.

It followed them.

The profanity that Gabe spat out let her know that he was aware of that as well. He reached for his gun, moving it on the seat next to him.

"Get down," he ordered.

Leigh debated it. After all, if those men started to shoot again, she would likely need to return fire—if she could remember how to do that. But Gabe didn't give her a choice. He caught onto the back of her neck and pushed her down on the seat. "I want you to stay down!"

She did, begrudgingly, but only because she figured he must have some kind of plan. "What now?" Leigh asked.

"We lose them."

He sounded so calm and confident—and so vague—but she saw the concern that had a hold on the muscles in his jaw. If these were the gunmen from the clinic, then they wouldn't give up easily, and losing them on an open highway might be next to impossible.

Leigh lifted her head just slightly so she could check the side mirror. The car was right behind them, and she thought she could see two people inside. No sign of any weapons, but that didn't mean they weren't armed.

"Hang on," Gabe let her know.

She barely had time to grab onto the armrest on the door when Gabe twisted the steering wheel and sent the truck barreling onto a narrow side road. It sent her sliding into him as well. There wasn't much space between them, and her cheek collided with his thigh.

When she moved away, Leigh fished through the gym bag that Jinx had given them and took out the extra magazines of ammunition so she could place them in her lap. She prayed they wouldn't need them.

"Stay down," Gabe warned again.

She glanced in the side mirror to see what had prompted him to reissue his order. Leigh saw someone in the car lowering the window. Moments later, she saw the man's hand. And the gun that he held.

Before she could even bring up her own weapon, Gabe took another hairpin turn. She peeked over the dash just as the truck bounced its way onto a dirt road. Gravel pummeled the tires and undercarriage, and dust seeped inside, causing her breath to clog even more than the fear had done.

Gabe dodged a scrub oak, its scraggly branches slapping against the window. Without taking his gaze from the path ahead, he cursed.

"Should I shoot at them?" she asked.

"No. Not yet."

Leigh braced herself for the bullets that she was sure the gunmen would fire into the truck.

But that didn't happen.

She lost sight of the car when Gabe took the next

two turns. He maneuvered onto a series of back roads and then cut through a narrow clearing that was lined with cedars and oaks. Whirling the steering wheel around, he circled them back in the other direction so they would face the car if it followed them. Just as quickly, he turned off the engine.

He didn't waste even a second of time. Gabe latched onto his gun, brought it up and braced his hand so that he was ready to fire. Leigh did the same. They were shoulder to shoulder, but since Gabe was left-handed, it didn't interfere with either of their aims.

And they waited.

The minutes crawled by. One by one. Leigh counted off the seconds in her head.

But there was no sign of the gunmen.

Either those men had given up, or else Gabe had truly managed to lose them. Leigh tried to pick through the sounds in the woods. The breeze rattling the leaves. The few birds that they hadn't scared off. What she didn't hear was the sound of a car engine.

Oh, God.

That frightened her even more than if she had heard one. Did that mean the gunmen had stopped and were now circling around from behind? Or was it possible they were on foot? Obviously, Gabe had already thought of that because she noticed his gaze darting all around them.

It made her wonder if they'd been in situations like this before. Possibly. After all, at one time she'd been an agent, too. Perhaps they had worked cases together.

That stirred something deep inside her. What exactly, she couldn't say. But even though the situation itself didn't feel familiar, the camaraderie, and the intimacy of it, certainly did.

Too familiar.

An image flashed through her mind. Not of gunmen or chases through the woods. It was an image of Gabe, naked. Beautifully naked. He had his hands on her. Their embrace was beyond intimate. The mental picture was so clear, so overwhelming, so erotic that Leigh gasped.

"What's wrong?" Gabe glanced around them, obviously looking for what had alarmed her.

"Nothing," she said on a rush of breath. "A memory, I think."

"Of what?"

She couldn't tell him. Leigh didn't even think she could get her mouth to say the words. She forced herself to think of the danger. The gunmen. It didn't completely wash away that image of Gabe, but it helped.

"How much longer do we wait?" she asked.

"Not long. If they were coming after us, they would have already done it." He started the truck again. "But cover us just in case. I'm getting us out of here."

Leigh didn't argue with that. She didn't want to stay in the woods any longer.

While Gabe maneuvered the truck through the path and back onto the dirt road, Leigh watched for any sign of the gunmen. It didn't disappoint her when she didn't see them, but it did create more questions in her mind.

"Why didn't they follow us, Gabe?"

"Maybe they didn't like the odds of coming at us head-on. I sure wouldn't have."

That made sense. Gabe had established high ground by the way he parked the truck, but high ground had merely given them a temporary advantage. It hadn't secured a victory. "That means they think they'll have a better opportunity to come at us later."

He made a sound of agreement. That didn't do a thing to ease the tension in her body. "So, is someone feeding them information as to our whereabouts?"

"Maybe," Gabe said quickly enough to indicate he'd already given the idea some thought. "Or maybe they're just lucky."

Leigh didn't think luck had a whole lot to do with this. "Could Jinx or Teresa Walters have let these guys know where we are?"

"Not Jinx. He's on our side, Leigh. And it's Teresa's job to find that cache of stolen weapons. I doubt she'd want to see what could be her star witness dead, especially since this case could lead to a promotion for her."

"That theory only works if Teresa isn't Dayton's accomplice." Leigh silently added Jinx into that equation, too. And anyone else that had anything to do with Dayton. Leigh had no idea how long a list that would be.

"I don't have a good feeling about either Jinx or

Teresa,'' Leigh continued. ''For now I'd prefer they not know where we are.''

Gabe didn't agree or disagree. He turned onto a paved road and sped up. ''So, what exactly did you remember back there, huh?''

Great. Just great. Of all the things they could discuss, why would he bring up that? She checked to make sure no one was following them—not that it was necessary. Leigh had hardly taken her attention away from the rearview mirror. Still, it gave her a moment to try to figure out what to say. And after a moment, she still had no clue how to answer him.

''Was it about us?'' Gabe asked.

Leigh nodded but didn't offer anything else. She took a deep breath when the same image flashed through her mind again. Good heavens, the man certainly had a beautiful body, or maybe she just had a good imagination. If so, then she also imagined that he had a tattoo on his right hip.

Gabe mumbled something under his breath. ''All right, if you won't answer, I'll fill in the blanks. We had some bad times along with the good ones. *Very* good ones. Yes, we argued, but with the exception of the last argument, we always made up. And yes, we loved each other enough to stand in front of a priest and take vows that we swore we'd never break.''

She was about to say that wasn't what she'd remembered—that it was nothing nearly as reverent as wedding vows and priests—but Gabe continued. ''We had all the hopes, dreams and problems of any other couple in love. We cared for each other." He cursed. "And yes, damn it, we even had great sex."

Bingo.

He must have sensed that he'd hit upon something. Maybe it was the change in the air that suddenly crackled between them. Or maybe it was just the look on her face. For whatever reason, he gave her a considering glance.

*"Great sex,"* he repeated, changing the inflection not from a comment to an assertion.

Leigh fought it, but the image stayed with her. The image of Gabe sliding his hands over her breasts. And lower. He touched her as if he knew every inch and every place of pleasure on her body.

He probably did.

And that was what Leigh had to push aside. She had no doubts that they'd had great sex, but it could have no part in what was going on now. They were in danger, and she wasn't even sure she trusted him.

"I won't get involved with you again," she said as if that answered everything. Now she only hoped her body understood the statement she'd just delivered.

"Are you trying to convince me or yourself?" he asked, that Texas drawl coming through and kissing each word.

The answer to that was easy.

Both.

GABE DIDN'T LIKE the silence he heard on the other end of the line. Teresa Walters hadn't said anything for a full five seconds. He knew that's how much time had passed because he'd counted.

He didn't want to count much longer.

It wasn't safe to hang around the Tip-Top gas station since those gunmen might still be in the area. It'd been nearly an hour and over fifty miles of back roads since he'd last seen that dark blue car, but he didn't want to wait around for it to return.

With the phone cradled against his shoulder, he glanced up when Leigh made her way out of the bathroom. She didn't dawdle, and several times she checked their surroundings. Obviously, she wasn't ready to let down her guard either.

"What makes you think Leigh's getting her memory back?" Teresa asked, paraphrasing what he'd told her all those seconds earlier.

"I don't *think* she's getting it back," Gabe assured her. He finished filling the gas tank and replaced the nozzle. He'd already paid the attendant in cash and was more than anxious to get out of there. "I know she is."

It was a lie. Or better yet, a test. He'd wanted to hear how Teresa would react to such news. Besides, Leigh had remembered something when they were in the truck. Just what he didn't know, but he would bet a month's paycheck that it was raunchy and involved sex. The look on her face had said loads about what had crossed her mind.

"What has she remembered exactly?" Teresa went on. "Does she know where her brother is?"

"No idea whatsoever. But she wants to find Philip as much as we do. I don't suppose you've learned anything?"

"Nothing. I'm having someone check to see if he's with his mother in England."

The chances of that were slim to none. Philip disliked his mother as much as Leigh did. That's the last place he would have gone. Unfortunately, that didn't narrow down their search area nearly enough.

"How about Dayton's accomplice?" Teresa again. "Does Leigh remember anything about that?"

"Not yet, but I don't think we'll have to wait too much longer." Leigh joined him and got back into the truck. "Her memory's coming back pretty fast."

Leigh's eyebrow arched. When he was done with the call, he'd have to explain this game of cat and mouse he was playing with Teresa. Then he'd have to remind Leigh that in the grand scheme of things, they were still the mice.

"All right," Teresa said as if he was about to deliver a decree, "where exactly are you now?"

"In Texas. At a place called Ed's Café."

Leigh's eyebrow rose again, and the corner of her mouth lifted in a half smile. Maybe he wouldn't have to explain things to her after all. It had to be fairly clear that he didn't intend to trust Agent Walters with their whereabouts, but Leigh had said right from the start that she didn't trust Teresa either. Gabe wasn't as convinced as she was, but it didn't hurt to be cautious.

"It's a mom-and-pop place near the I–10," he added for Teresa's benefit.

Even as he told that additional lie, Gabe glanced at the sign that said Tip-Top Gas. *Louisiana Hospitality* was in fading red letters just below that. And the place wasn't anywhere near the interstate.

"See if you can find out who followed us, will you, Teresa?" Gabe asked, and he gave her the car's license-plate numbers. The *real* numbers. With some luck, and if she was so inclined, she might be able to find out who was after them. It was a long shot, but Gabe had gotten lucky with long shots before.

"Will do," Teresa assured him. "You stay put, and I'll have someone out to you in a couple of hours."

"Sounds good." Or it sounded like a trap. If so, it'd be a trap that wasn't anywhere near Leigh and him.

Leigh handed him a bottle of water from the cooler when he put away his phone. "That was Teresa," he let her know.

"I heard." She got some water for herself. "What will you do if it turns out that she's the one behind this?"

"Then I'll deal with her." And speaking of dealing with unpleasant things, there was something else he should have already checked. Gabe cursed himself for not handling the whole situation better. "I need to find out if you're wearing a transmitter."

The bottle of water stopped halfway to her mouth. "A what?"

"A tracking device that would allow someone to follow us. While you were in the bathroom, I checked my clothes and shoes. Now I need to check yours."

Alarm and maybe something else flashed through her eyes. Gabe didn't want to hope that other flash was a result of what she'd recalled earlier.

"I'll check my own clothes," she let him know. "Why don't you go through the gym bag?"

"It's clean. Jinx put it together himself." Of course, she knew that, and that's why she'd suggested it. For whatever reason, she didn't trust Jinx.

"Why don't you check it anyway?" She put her water aside and felt around the pockets of her shorts. "So, exactly what am I looking for anyway?"

"A device about the thickness of a penny and a third the size."

He hadn't meant to watch her do a clothes check, but he rather liked the idea of watching Leigh run her hands over her body. It reminded him of the times she'd done the same to him. And vice versa.

She patted and felt around every inch of her clothes and finally shrugged. "Nothing."

"Hand me your shoes."

Gabe looked carefully at the flip-flops but saw nothing. He shook his head and handed them back to her.

"Maybe it's on the truck," she suggested. "Or maybe there isn't one at all."

The truck was out—Jinx would have already checked for such things, using the best equipment the Bureau had to offer. But it was possible those gunmen had just gotten lucky. Gabe, however, didn't want to rely on that. In fact, if he'd been thinking straight, he should have done this search the night before when they were in the bayou. It might have saved them that latest run for their lives.

He studied Leigh carefully, looking for possible hiding places. After all, there'd been a good hour where she was out of his sight when they were at the clinic. The doctor, MRI technician, Jinx and Teresa had all been with her at various times, and it was possible the doctor had been on the wrong payroll. Or maybe Teresa hadn't wanted to take any chances with Leigh getting away from her.

"Lean forward," he told her. Gabe climbed onto the seat next to her and reached for the bandage on her forehead.

"You think there's a transmitter in my bandage?"

"Only one way to find out." As gently as he could, he peeled off the tape. No transmitter, but there were some angry-looking stitches and a bruise covering a good portion of the side of her forehead. It turned his stomach to see that on her. It reminded him of the monster they were up against. A monster he very much wanted to deal with when the time came.

Gabe was actually looking forward to delivering some payback.

"What is it?" she asked, obviously seeing his alarm.

"Nothing." He quickly replaced the bandage and reached for her foot.

She gave him a puzzled glance. ''So, why did you tell Teresa I'd gotten my memory back?''

Oh, that. He'd figured Leigh would want to know about that conversation, especially since he hadn't given her any warning about what he'd planned to say. ''It wasn't a complete lie.'' As he'd done with the bandage on her forehead, he lifted back the tape and began to unwind the layers of gauze on her ankle. ''Of course, I doubt you'd be willing to share with me exactly what you remembered, huh?''

''No.''

It wasn't hard to see the deer-caught-in-a-headlight glaze in her eyes, and that told Gabe loads. ''It was about sex,'' he concluded.

Her chin came up. ''Is that all you think about?''

Gabe saw right through her—that insolent reply wasn't a very good smoke screen. There was a veneer barely covering the slick layer of emotions just beneath the surface. Something about that memory had shaken her.

But what?

And why the heck did he feel this overwhelming need to find out?

She must have sensed that she couldn't fool him because she glanced away. ''I'm not even sure it was a memory. It could have been...something I saw in a movie.''

He seriously doubted it. Movie memories didn't cause people to blush, and that's what she was doing. ''Tell me about it, and I'll let you know.''

Leigh hesitated. And hesitated. She began to nibble on her bottom lip. "Do you have a tattoo of a longhorn on your lower right hip?"

It probably wasn't a good time to smile, but Gabe just couldn't help himself. He nodded and continued to unwrap her bandage. "It's a relic from a trip that my uncle and I took to Mexico for my eighteenth birthday. The only way you could have seen that was if I'd been naked."

She nodded almost begrudgingly.

Gabe laughed before he could stop himself. "We were married, Leigh. *Are* married," he corrected. "Trust me, we got naked more than a couple of times. It doesn't surprise me that you'd remember one of them. Just please tell me I was doing something memorable and not disgusting like drooling on my pillow."

Her mouth quivered as if she was fighting back a smile of her own. "You definitely weren't drooling. But I think maybe I was."

There was the sense of humor that he missed. God, did he miss it. It made him ache to know he'd gone so long without it. Without her.

Her eyes lifted to his, and he saw all the things Leigh was feeling. She obviously didn't want this heat simmering between them. Neither did he. Yet, neither of them seemed to have what it took to stop it.

There was a moment when he thought he could talk himself out of what he was about to do. That moment came and went. Then Gabe leaned in and brushed his mouth over hers. It sent a jolt through his body, and the memories of the taste of her came flooding back.

She didn't move away when his mouth came to hers again. Their lips touched. Barely. At first. But it didn't stay that way. Her mouth was warm and yielding. Gabe took it before he could stop himself.

Her scent curled around him. There were undertones of her arousal. Subtle. Yet not subtle to his own body.

Gabe hesitated a moment to see if she would stop him. She didn't. It was Leigh who deepened the kiss. Leigh who adjusted her position on the seat and wound her arms around him. The contact brought her right against his chest. He felt the softness of her breasts, and the hardness of her nipples, which were obviously puckered and drawn from the contact. What was left of his resolve when right out the window.

Lowering his hand, he slipped his fingertips over her nipples and had the pleasure of hearing her moan in response. He was pretty sure he moaned as well.

"Leigh," he whispered against her mouth.

She gave it right back to him. She said his name. A whisper. A plea. An invitation. He couldn't accept it, of course, but with each passing moment, it got harder and harder for him to remember why they needed to stop.

He heard the ringing sound in his ears, but it took Gabe a moment to realize it was his phone and not his body's reaction to Leigh.

Hell. He'd obviously lost his mind. He had forgotten where he was and what had happened just minutes earlier. Here he was parked in front of a gas station kissing her. For about a million reasons, he shouldn't be doing that.

She made a sound of frustration that he understood all too well and eased away from him. Gabe did his own easing, knowing he had to put some distance between them.

Before he answered the call, he glanced around to make sure they were still alone. Thank God they appeared to be. The only person nearby was the attendant inside, who still had his face stuck in a magazine. Still, Gabe didn't plan to take any more chances with her life. He hoped the look he gave Leigh assured her of that.

He fished the phone out of the gym bag and brought it to his ear.

"Gabe? It's Frank Templeton." The man's voice was frantic and hardly more than a ragged whisper.

"Frank?" Gabe repeated. "How'd you get this number?"

"Jinx. I called him and convinced him that I'd talk to only you."

Gabe didn't know what to think about that. He hoped Jinx hadn't made a mistake by doing that. Of course, he did need to speak to Frank. He just hadn't expected it to happen over the phone. "Where are you?"

"I'd rather not say. I just want to make sure you'll be at the house tomorrow night?"

"I'll be there." Hopefully alone while Leigh waited

in the truck. The only other person who knew about that meeting was Jinx, and Gabe wanted to keep things that way.

"Good. I have to talk to you. Listen, I can't stay on the line long, but you need to find Leigh. She's in a lot of danger."

Gabe certainly didn't need anyone to tell him that, but he played along, not wanting to send Frank deeper into hiding. "Why do you say that?"

"I don't have all the details, but I should have it worked out by tomorrow night. If you find Leigh by then, bring her with you so I can talk to her about that disk we found two years ago. I think that's what started all of this. And Gabe? Don't trust anyone on the task force. That's why I've been on the run. Somebody's out to kill me and maybe Leigh, too."

Oh, yeah. Definitely. But he wasn't sure that threat was coming from the task force. "Why would someone want to kill you?"

"I don't know. A cover-up maybe. I think it has something to do with those confiscated weapons that should have been destroyed and weren't. I have to go, Gabe."

Just like that, the line went dead. Gabe wasn't sure if the man had hung up voluntarily or if someone had cut his phone line. Either way, he obviously wouldn't get a chance to ask Frank a few more questions.

"Was that Frank Templeton?" Leigh asked.

"Yes. He's alive, but he sounds like a man who knows that he's in a whole lot of danger." Gabe turned off the phone and tossed it back in the gym bag. He couldn't waste any more time. He lifted Leigh's foot into his lap and continued to check the bandage for the transmitter.

Leigh leaned forward and looked into the gauze layers as well. "We're still meeting him tomorrow night, right?"

"Yeah." Hell or high water wouldn't stop that meeting. It would be dangerous, no doubt about it, but he didn't see another way around it. Frank probably wouldn't want to relay sensitive information over the phone. "This shouldn't come as a surprise, but Frank said you were in danger and that I shouldn't let you out of my sight."

Gabe figured that was advice he would most certainly take. It might significantly improve Leigh's chances of getting out of this situation alive.

Hurrying up his search, he continued to go through the bandage. He didn't find the transmitter until he got to the last of the gauzy layers. Just the sight of it made him curse. It was a chilling, hard reminder that he'd been stupid and that stupidity just might cost them everything.

Using the tip of his little finger, Gabe lifted out the tiny transmitter and inspected it. Too bad he couldn't send the device to the crime lab to have it checked out, but there wasn't time for that. In fact, there wasn't much time for him to do anything. He tossed it out the window and quickly started the truck.

''We have to put some distance between us and that thing,'' he let Leigh know.

He didn't waste another precious second either. He pulled away from the gas station and sped up. Thanks to his lapse in judgment, he'd have to cover their tracks before he could even think about heading to Grand Valley. Gabe sure as heck didn't want anyone following them there.

''You mean I've been running around with that transmitter in my bandage this whole time?'' She pressed down the edges of the tape that held the gauze strips in place. ''Who put it there? And who had access to me before I regained consciousness?''

''Too many people,'' Gabe provided.

''Who?'' she persisted.

''Well, the doctor and the technician who did your MRI.'' Gabe took a deep breath. ''And a couple of times Jinx and Teresa were with you, too.''

He was sure Leigh would have had an opinion about that. But she didn't have time to voice it. All hell broke loose.

A bullet came crashing through the back window.

# *Chapter Eight*

"Get down!" Gabe's voice echoed through the truck.

Leigh did as he said, dropping to the floor in a split second, but she had no intentions of staying down. Memory or no memory, she still had her instincts, and her instincts for survival were pretty strong. She certainly wasn't going to give up without a fight. She latched onto her gun and came up prepared to fire.

"Damn it, Leigh. I said get down."

Another bullet skipped off the roof of the truck, gashing through the metal. "Why? So you can be the sole target for whoever's trying to kill us? I'm not an invalid, so don't go all macho on me now."

She ignored his profanity-laced objection and stretched her hand toward the door. She rolled the window halfway down, all the while trying to stay low in the seat.

Leigh didn't know exactly what she planned to do, but she thought she might try shooting at the car tires. Using the small sliding window on the back was out—it had become a webby sheet of fractured safety glass when the bullet slammed into it. It was a chilling reminder of how close Gabe and she had come to getting killed.

"Climb over here and drive," Gabe snarled. "I'll return fire."

Leigh wanted to argue with that order, but she didn't want to try to win an argument at the cost of dying. It would only take one of those bullets to do either one of them in. Besides, she didn't even know if she was a good shot.

Gabe was.

He'd proven that back at the clinic.

Changing places was easier said than done, and they no doubt made clear targets while trying to do that. At Gabe's direction, she maneuvered her body across his, and he tried to slip beneath hers. They did all that while he kept his foot on the accelerator and while Leigh steered.

"Under different circumstances, I might consider this foreplay," he mumbled.

"You probably consider breathing foreplay," Leigh countered in a mumble of her own.

Gabe made a sound, part laughter, part frustration, all nerves.

There was another sputter of bullets. One of them took out a chunk of the mirror on the driver's side. Once Gabe was out of the way, Leigh floored the accelerator, watching the speedometer quickly go over eighty. The older-model truck probably wouldn't do much more than that, but she continued to press, knowing she had to put some distance between them and that car.

Gabe plundered through the gym bag and retrieved the extra magazines of ammunition. They were right where Leigh had placed them only minutes earlier. It wasn't quite an arsenal, but they could probably hold their own.

For a while anyway.

She glanced in what was left of the side mirror as Gabe aimed the gun out the window and fired several shots. Since they all appeared to be direct hits, and since the car windows didn't shatter, she guessed that the glass was bulletproof.

Sweet heaven. The gunmen had truly come prepared for a shoot-out.

"For God's sakes, Leigh, keep your head low," Gabe yelled when he glanced over at her.

"That's what I'm trying to do." She slid as deep in the seat as she could and took the truck around a sharp curve in the road. "Can't you shoot out their tires or something?" she asked impatiently.

"That's what I had in mind," Gabe said with equal impatience.

The barrel of a gun snaked out of the front passenger's window and rattled off more bullets. Gabe returned fire, and one of the bullets hit his opponent's weapon, sending a spark from metal colliding with metal.

Without hesitating, Gabe sent several rounds slightly farther to the right, and even with the distance between the vehicles, Leigh could see that he'd hit the gunman's shooting arm.

Gabe didn't let up. With the one gunman at least partially out of commission, Gabe leaned out the window and sent a barrage of bullets into the other vehicle. He must have hit something, or caused enough distraction, because the blue sedan clipped the ditch, the right tires dipping into some sloshy mud.

The driver swerved, trying to maneuver the car back onto the road. He wasn't successful. Gabe aimed his pistol at the tires and fired. And fired. And fired. The rubber on the tires disintegrated, unraveling until the driver had no choice but to grind to a stop.

Leigh didn't waste any time. She sped away, praying those men wouldn't get themselves out of that ditch anytime soon.

"Any sign they had backup?" She was almost afraid to hear Gabe's answer. The last thing she wanted was to go another round with yet another set of gunmen. Her whole body was a tangle of nerves and adrenaline.

"No. I think they were alone." But that obviously didn't make Gabe let down his guard. He kept his weapon aimed and his attention focused on the road.

"They must have found us by using that transmitter," she said more to herself than Gabe. "Or else Teresa somehow traced the call—"

"Teresa didn't put this attempted hit together."

"But you were just talking to her on the phone,"

Leigh pointed out. In fact, it appeared to her that Teresa was the most likely suspect.

"She wouldn't have had time to trace the call and dispatch someone that fast. These guys were right on our tail all along. My guess is they would have gotten to us even sooner if they hadn't had to navigate their way around these country roads. No. They had their orders long before I made that call to Teresa. That stop we made at the gas station just gave them time to catch up with us."

Gabe had obviously given it plenty of thought. Good. Maybe that meant he had a plan to put an end to this. Leigh didn't want to play hide-and-seek any longer with people who wanted her dead.

"Where to now?" she asked when she saw the sign for the approaching westbound interstate. It was the direction they needed to go to get to Frank Templeton in Grand Valley, but it would put them out in the open on a major highway.

Gabe never even hesitated. "We can't take the interstate, and we need to get off this road, especially since they know what vehicle we're in."

He turned around in the seat and reached out the still-lowered window to give his mirror an adjustment—probably so he could still do a visual check in case anyone else followed them. It was a reminder that even though she'd put some miles between the gunmen and them, they weren't out of immediate danger yet.

"So, where do we go if not to Grand Valley?" Leigh asked.

Again, he didn't hesitate. "I thought about the cabin back in the bayou."

It took her a moment to figure out what he meant. "You mean the place that Jinx owns?"

He nodded. "It might be safe there."

Safe, yes, in many ways. But Leigh remembered what Gabe had said about that cabin.

It was the place where they'd spent their honeymoon.

That shouldn't have bothered her. After all, this time they certainly wouldn't be going there to do honeymoonish things. They would be going there to get away from the gunmen. Still, there was something about the idea that made her pulse start to race again.

Leigh prayed it was racing because of the potential danger and nothing else.

"There's just one problem with going all the way out to Jinx's cabin," Gabe continued. "Tomorrow, we'd have a lot of miles to cover to get back to Grand Valley. Of course, we don't have to be there until midnight."

But it would mean a lot of extra time on the roads. Besides, for reasons Leigh didn't want to explore, she didn't think it was a good idea to spend the night there alone with Gabe. "Is there anyplace else we could go—a place that wouldn't involve Jinx?"

Or Jinx's knowledge of their whereabouts. Now, that was something Leigh didn't mind exploring. She really didn't want anyone to know where they were, but especially Jinx and Teresa Walters. If they went to his cabin, he might very well find out they were there.

"There is a place. A house." Gabe paused. Then he shrugged. "It's about fifty miles north of Houston. It's not that far from Grand Valley."

Houston. That got her full attention. There was a tiny flutter in her heart. A warm tingle worked its way from that flutter all the way to her stomach. "So, what is this place—an FBI safe house?"

"It's the house where I grew up."

The flutter got significantly worse. His home. "Your family will be there?" she asked hesitantly.

He shook his head. "My folks moved to Brownsville a few years back so they could help take care of my grandparents. I've got a brother, Reese, who's in the air force stationed over in Florida. My sister, Maria, is married and lives in Sacramento." He took a deep breath. "Dad talks about selling the ranch, but he just hasn't gotten around to it."

Yet more pieces of her past that she didn't remember—she had in-laws. Apparently lots of them. Gabe's family. Leigh had been so preoccupied with various aspects of her own life that she hadn't thought to ask Gabe about his.

"So, we're both from Texas," she commented. "Then, how did we end up in New Orleans?"

He gathered up the extra ammunition and returned

it to the gym bag. "We were both assigned there five years ago."

And that's where they'd obviously met. Fallen in love. Married. And then had fallen out of love.

Or something.

She glanced at him. He was still in a vigilant mode with his attention on the side mirror. She'd seen him like this before, of course. At the clinic and again that morning when Jinx came walking up to them in the bayou. But there was something about his formidable expression that made her go back for a second look.

And a third.

It was probably a weird hormonal reaction, but there was something appealing about that wariness. But Gabe didn't especially need to be on alert to be considered attractive. He was, well, hot. No doubt about it. It wasn't difficult for her to see why she'd been attracted to him in the first place.

Leigh cleared her throat. Best to put those kind of thoughts aside. Far, far aside. "How long will it take us to get to the house?"

"About four or five hours. We'll take the back roads so I can make sure no one is following us."

Of course, he'd want to make sure of that. She wanted the same thing. She also wanted her heart rate to go back to normal, but it didn't seem as if that would happen in the next couple of hours. Leigh couldn't blame that entirely on the gunmen. It had plenty to do with that ill-timed, stupid kissing session that had gone on in the truck right before the bullets started flying.

Knowing she shouldn't put it off, Leigh broached the difficult subject. "We have to talk about that kiss—"

"Yeah, we do," he interrupted. "It shouldn't have happened."

She hadn't expected him to agree with her. Well, maybe she had. No one with a fully functioning brain could have thought that was a good thing for them to be kissing with all the danger lurking about. But she hadn't expected Gabe to voice that agreement so easily. After all, he was the one who'd started it.

Technically.

Admittedly, there was nothing technical about her participation.

"I'm sorry I let things go that far," she added. "I mean, it was just a physical response. And everything is all muddled up in my head." God, she was rambling. Why did her nerves suddenly feel so close to the surface? "I just didn't want you to read anything into it. Because I didn't."

He made a sound that could have meant nothing. Or anything. "Be honest, Leigh. Do you really think you could have done something to stop that kiss?"

Not that one, specifically. The heat of the moment had taken hold of her and hadn't been especially receptive to letting go. That didn't mean she would let the heat take over again. It was just a matter of her not letting herself get caught off guard.

Leigh took a deep breath, hoping it would help her come up with an answer to his question. It didn't. She settled for the easiest way out. "This isn't the right time for us to work out our personal problems, okay?"

"And you think by saying it, all of this heat simmering between us will just go away?" Gabe didn't wait for her to answer. "It won't, you know. Personal problems or not, it was there the first time we laid eyes on each other."

"Maybe, but even you should be able to see the logic in us not acting on this...heat."

"Of course I do," Gabe readily agreed. He scrubbed his hand over his face. "Look, I don't want to get involved again with you either."

That was exactly what she wanted to hear, but it made her throat turn to dust. She didn't even attempt to say anything. Leigh just kept driving while Gabe continued.

"When you left two years ago, I promised I'd never let myself care for you again." He mumbled something in Spanish under his breath. Definitely profanity. Leigh understood most of it, and it wasn't mild. "That's a promise I *will* keep. My job is to stop those gunmen from hurting you and find out who's behind these attacks. That's all."

"Yes," she agreed, a little alarmed that he sounded so adamant. And angry. She was just a job to him. Leigh had known that all along, but it was a shock to hear it spelled out for her. A few ill-timed kisses certainly wouldn't have changed that.

As if he'd declared war on it, Gabe checked the magazine in his gun. "Those vows that you threw away two years ago will just have to stay where you threw them because I don't intend to go there again, understand?"

All right. So, that was a little more honesty than she'd expected. Or wanted. "Then we agree. We shouldn't get involved again."

"Yeah, we agree."

For what it was worth, it seemed they'd reached a compromise. Sort of. But since his jaw muscles were battling each other, Leigh guessed that it wasn't an amicable one for him.

She told herself to leave well enough alone, but she didn't take her own advice. "Why did I leave you? Did I have an affair or something?" But Leigh knew it wasn't that. She just didn't know how she knew it.

"No affair," he confirmed several long moments later. He scraped his thumbnail over a ragged patch of leather on the dash. What he didn't do was look at her. "You came to me with information you'd learned about Dayton," he said slowly. "I'd known him for years. He was a friend. And I didn't think he was capable of doing something like that."

"But the proof—"

"I thought the proof was wrong, that someone had doctored the evidence."

"Certainly not me?" That didn't feel right either, but there was something about this explanation that stirred other emotions. Other sensations. Anger. Hurt.

Pain. Betrayal. The emotions slowly began to unravel inside her.

"No. But I thought someone had," he explained. "You were equally sure of Dayton's guilt. A feeling, you said. A feeling I dismissed because I thought he was someone I knew and trusted."

In other words, Gabe had made a mistake. Leigh didn't need her memory to know he wouldn't have handled that well. But then, neither had she. "Did you confront Dayton?"

Gabe nodded. "He came to me and said he was innocent. I believed him. I told him that I'd do whatever I could to clear his name. I even went to Jinx and convinced him to investigate further before they brought Dayton in. Just the hint of impropriety would have destroyed his career in the Justice Department."

Okay. That probably would have happened. "Since I already believed Dayton was guilty, I suppose we argued?"

"We most certainly would have…if Dayton hadn't tried to kill you."

"He what?"

This time the profanity wasn't quite so muffled. "He tried to make it look a carjacking. He shot you in the arm and then chased you down an alley. Dayton would have killed you if a bystander hadn't stepped in. When he realized the game was over, he turned the gun on himself."

Leigh didn't remember any of it, but she could almost see those images in her mind and she could feel the raw emotions that went along with them. Not easy sensations to grasp.

"You nearly died because I trusted the wrong man." Gabe glanced at her, for only a second, before he turned back to the window.

This was probably one of the few times that amnesia was a good thing. Even though Leigh had hints of the horrible events that had gone on, her lack of memory forced her to look at them objectively.

"I was wrong to say you threw away your vows," he added several moments later. "I gave you a damn good reason to throw them away."

Maybe. But all the little pieces to this puzzle just didn't add up. She would have been angry and hurt that Gabe hadn't trusted her, but why would that have caused her to walk away from her job, their marriage and him?

There had to be something else.

But what?

Maybe it was simply that she knew Dayton did indeed have an accomplice, and she didn't want to take unnecessary chances with her life. But why wouldn't she have turned to Gabe or even Jinx to help her? One was her husband. The other, supposedly their close friend. With their combined FBI training, the three of them could have almost certainly flushed out an accomplice who might want her dead.

So, if her sudden, unexplained departure wasn't solely the result of the Dayton fiasco, then what had it all been about? And better yet—did Gabe know what had caused her to leave?

Maybe.

And if he did, why did he feel the need to keep it from her?

Leigh mulled those questions over while she drove toward the Texas state line.

## Chapter Nine

Gabe put the rest of their take-out chicken in the fridge and finished off one of the bottles of Mexican beer he'd found on the bottom shelf. Obviously, his folks came back often enough to keep the place stocked and clean.

The house was one big giant memory. Not all of it was good either. In fact, some of those memories were downright unpleasant.

Rather than reliving the past, he focused on the fact that it was a safe place to spend the night and trade out vehicles. He'd left his college clunker in the garage ten years earlier when he'd left for the FBI Academy. Thankfully, his father had seen to it over the years, and it started right up. Gabe just hoped the vehicle got them to Grand Valley so they could meet with Frank Templeton.

The old pipes in the house groaned and creaked when Leigh turned on the faucet in the bathroom. Since the only bathroom was just off the kitchen, he had no trouble hearing the rattle of the shower curtain when she stepped inside the tub. He also had no trouble imagining how she looked with the water cascading down her naked body.

Of course, Gabe had an advantage with that particular image—he'd seen Leigh naked in the shower many times. Even in this one.

And on many occasions he'd joined her.

Cursing himself and his too-good memory, Gabe got himself another beer and sat down at the kitchen table. He'd have to tell his family, of course, about Leigh's return. He just didn't know what that telling would include. They knew little of Leigh's and his breakup, only that she'd left the Bureau to make her life elsewhere. Now he'd have to explain something he didn't have a real explanation for himself.

He took a long drink of his beer and stared at the ceiling. There probably wasn't one room in the entire house where at one time or another she hadn't told him *I love you.* In those days before the incident with Joe Dayton, Leigh had been generous with those three words. And they hadn't just been words. She'd meant them. It was impossible to fake feelings that ran that deep. Gabe knew. Because he'd said those words right back to her.

Riled at himself for remembering that, he took out his phone and pressed in the numbers for a call he should have made hours earlier.

"Who are you calling?" he heard Leigh ask.

He turned so quickly, he nearly fell out of his chair. She was in the doorway that led from the hall into the kitchen. Not naked, of course. She wore a robe she'd borrowed from his mother's closet. It was several sizes too large for her, but that didn't stop Gabe from noticing the way the sash cinched around her waist.

"Jinx," he answered.

Her eyebrow arched. "Why?"

"Because he'll want to know that we're all right. I'm sure Teresa's already contacted him so he'll know there were gunmen after us."

Her hair was still wet. It lay against the sides of her face and neck. When she stepped into the room, she brought the scent of her shower with her.

She smelled like gardenias. Something subtle but potent. The timing was lousy, but it went straight through him like wildfire. Of course, just being close to her had a way of doing that. The two years they'd spent apart had done nothing to diminish the raw passion she ignited within him.

Gabe didn't dare get up from that chair. For one thing, he couldn't. Well, not without settling down his own body first. But he also didn't need to be any closer to her. He decided it was a good time to make that call, so he pressed in the last of the numbers.

"I'd rather Jinx didn't know where we are," Leigh added.

Gabe was about to assure her, again, that they could trust Jinx, but he didn't have time because he heard his friend's voice on the other end of the line.

"It's me." Gabe paused, wondering what to add to that. "We're safe."

"Thank God. How bad did things get?"

"Bad enough. We're going to lay low for the night."

He glanced at Leigh. She still had that look in her eyes—the one that questioned his judgment. Maybe she was thinking about another man he'd trusted. Joe Dayton. A friend who'd turned out not to be a friend after all. But Jinx wasn't Joe Dayton. Gabe knew he could trust this man. Still, there was no reason to let anyone know where they were. That would perhaps give Leigh some peace of mind.

"We should make it to Grand Valley in plenty of time," Gabe continued. "You'll be there?"

"Wouldn't miss it. I'll stay back though. I don't want Frank to see me and get spooked."

That was a good plan. Gabe didn't know Frank Templeton that well, but he certainly seemed like the type who'd spook easily. Of course, in this case Frank perhaps had a reason for it. The same person who'd gone after them would likely go after Frank as well. If he or she could find Frank, that is.

"See you tomorrow." Gabe turned off the phone before Jinx could ask anything else—especially anything about their location.

Leigh leaned against the wall next to the refrigerator. "Thanks for not telling him where we are."

Gabe nodded and tipped his head to the beer. "You want one?"

"No, thanks. But I wouldn't mind another cup of that coffee." She walked to the old-fashioned drip coffeepot on the stove and refilled the earthenware mug she'd left on the counter. As Gabe knew she would, she added three heaping teaspoons of sugar.

Leigh drank several sips before she continued. "I found some clothes in that back bedroom that look like they'll fit me. If you don't mind, I'll borrow them for the trip tomorrow."

"Of course." They were probably some old things Maria had left behind when she left home for college. Hopefully, the fit wouldn't be as distracting as the shorts and top had been. If so, he might have to borrow some blinders from the barn to keep himself from being too distracted.

"I noticed the pictures in your parents' room. I didn't recognized them," Leigh added almost as an apology. "But they look like nice people."

"They are."

She fidgeted with some chili-shaped salt and pepper shakers on the counter. "So, was this place part of a working ranch before your folks moved to Brownsville?"

When she pushed her hand through her hair, Gabe glanced at her. Her nerves were definitely showing. Hell, his probably were, too. There was nothing relaxing about this conversation.

"Yeah. There's about two hundreds acres total. The land has been in the Sanchez family for three generations. I think that's why my father is reluctant to sell it, even though none of the kids have ranching in their blood. I guess he figures either Reese or I will change our minds.''

The room suddenly seemed too warm. Gabe got up and raised the window over the sink. The night air was more muggy than cool, and it began to spill into the room, bringing the scents of Texas with it. The pasture grass. The wildflowers. His mother's roses that were in full bloom. Even with all that, he could still detect Leigh's own unique scent.

Rather than stare at his wife, Gabe stared out into the darkness instead.

''There are four children in the photos in the bedroom,'' she said. ''Two girls and two boys. I thought you said you only had one sister.''

Hell. The woman sure could zone in on the worst of subjects. He bracketed his hands on the counter. ''My other sister, Emily, died when she was just a kid.''

''Oh.'' He heard the sympathy, and yet another apology in her voice. She cleared her throat and thankfully changed the subject. ''Tell me about this house in Grand Valley where we're meeting Frank.''

''It'll take us about a couple hours to get there.'' Thankfully, they had some time since they didn't have to meet him until the following night. Maybe nothing else would go wrong between now and then.

''There'll be guards?'' she asked.

''There shouldn't be.'' He shook his head. ''I have no way of knowing if Frank called anyone else, but it didn't sound as if he'd trust too many people.''

Despite the fact he knew it was a stupid thing to do, Gabe looked at her again. Hell. How could anyone look that good wearing an old chenille robe? "Listen, I know the adrenaline might still have you pumped, but you need to get some rest. We'll have plenty to do if Frank comes through tomorrow night. If he can tell us who Dayton's accomplice is, then we'll have to get that information to someone who won't kill us just because we have it."

"Any idea who we can trust with that?" She drank more of her coffee.

"Jinx. He'll find a way to get it into the right hands. That's why I want him to meet us there. We'll have to get Frank out of the area tomorrow night. He won't be safe there very long."

"No, I don't suspect he will." Worry lines bunched up her forehead. She set the coffee mug back on the table and slid the tip of her index finger around the rim. Gabe found the gesture, well, erotic. Of course, almost anything she could have done would have been erotic. He definitely had a one-track mind tonight.

Knowing he had to say, or do, something, he motioned toward the bandage on her foot. "How are the stitches?"

"As good as can be expected." She took a deep breath that forced her breasts against the tightly cinched fabric of the robe. "I changed the bandages and used some of that antibiotic cream from the first-aid kit."

"Good." And that was all he managed to get out.

Her gaze came to his. Slowly. As if she was fighting the moment as much as he was. There was a hint of panic in her sea-green eyes and something else, something familiar.

Something that immediately kicked his body into overdrive.

Gabe forgot all about her amnesia and the mess they were in. He forgot all about the hurt, the anger, the pain and the fact that just hours earlier he'd sworn never to get involved with her again.

All he remembered was that Leigh was his wife.

And he wanted her.

Gabe reached out and grabbed onto fists full of that god-awful robe and wrenched her closer. She didn't resist, didn't even mutter an objection. There were no more preliminaries, no long yearning looks, no soft caressing breaths. Just them. Two people who obviously needed each other.

Starving, he took her mouth—because it was his for the taking. He could feel every nerve in his body. And hers. The tension drummed through his pulse, slicing through him with both pleasure and pain. The sheer need he had for her nearly brought him to his knees.

Her breath caught when he turned her and backed her against the sink. Gabe wasn't even sure if he was breathing. Everything seemed to swirl around them.

"We should stop this," he somehow managed to say. "So, now would be a good time to do it...unless you want it to continue."

She just stared at him, her warm, moist breath hitting against a rather sensitive spot on his neck.

"Well?" he asked. "Yes or no?"

Leigh caught onto his shoulders and pulled him to her. "Yes."

SHE'D OBVIOUSLY LOST her mind. She'd said yes. Yes! How could she have possibly said that? Still, Leigh kissed him as if he were the source of her next breath.

With the fresh, tangled emotions rocketing through her, she pulled back. Slightly. And tried to get control of herself. She saw something in the depth of Gabe's midnight-blue eyes that caused her heart to jolt. She saw the need and knew without a doubt that it was the same need reflected in her own eyes.

She pulled in her breath. This wasn't about passion, or sex. It wasn't the time for her hormones to start raging. Yet she felt helpless against the mighty force that had apparently already been set into motion.

Somewhere through the haze, it occurred to her again that she should stop and regroup. Things were spinning out of control.

"Gabe," she whispered. It was a warning. And a plea. A fear. And a necessity. All of the things that she'd tried to tamp down rose to the surface.

And escaped.

In what seemed to be a burst of fire, his mouth came to hers, and he kissed her. It was rough. Almost punishing. But she knew it couldn't have been any gentler.

The connection between them wouldn't have allowed anything less than what he gave her.

Digging her fingers into his shoulders, she snapped him to her so the hard muscles of his body pressed right into her. The fit was so perfect, so good, that her eyes watered. And her heart soared.

He didn't break the kiss, but Gabe fisted a hand in her hair and maneuvered her so that the small of her back pressed against the sink. Without it, and his arm to support her, she would have no doubt fallen.

He took his clever mouth to her neck, and then to the spot just beneath her ear. They'd obviously spent a long time kissing because Gabe seemed to know every pleasure point and erogenous zone on her body. He evidently remembered which ones would turn her to instant flames.

His lips brushed against her earlobe. It didn't stay a brush though. He flicked his tongue over it. Sucked it. Lingered with his hot, moist breath until she wanted to wrap herself around him and beg for more.

Still, she could have perhaps stopped at that point if it'd just been the kiss. It wasn't. While he continued the assault on her ear, he slid his hand over her throat. And then lower into the V-opening of the robe. His fingertips found her nipples and brought them to hard peaks.

"Yes," she whispered.

At the sound of her voice, he eased back and looked at her. His eyes were hot and narrowed. The intensity should have frightened her, but she was beyond that. Beyond fear. Beyond reason.

She didn't even try to stop him when he reached for the sash that held the robe together. He undid it and eased one side off her shoulder.

"I'm going to kiss you there," he let her know, his fingertips fondling her nipple.

She heard the primitive sound claw its way past his throat, felt the slow, eating hunger in his touch. And she was lost. Willingly lost.

Gabe did as he promised. He lowered his head and claimed her breast, first one and then the other, much as he'd already claimed her mouth. Leigh leaned into him and let herself fall into the fiery haze of passion and need.

It was that need that sent her searching for relief. Leigh rubbed herself against him. Seeking. Needing something that only Gabe could give her. His thigh grazed the feverish center of her body, and the brief contact made her gasp.

That seemed to be the only encouragement Gabe needed to up the ante. He slid his rough, callused hand down her body and to her thigh.

"Don't look away," he insisted when she started to close her eyes. "I've waited a long time to be with you like this. I want to see what it does to you."

Leigh couldn't have refused if she'd wanted. She held his gaze, somehow. Even when he skimmed his hand to the back of her knee. He lifted it, positioning it, until it tucked against the outside of his thigh.

Still, she watched.

Her breath shattered when his hand began to move again. He took his time. Inch by precious inch. Just his fingertips brushing over her skin as he made his way from her knee. To her thigh. And then to her stomach.

"Since the moment you came back, I've ached to touch you like this." His voice was hoarse and hardly more than a whisper.

Yes. She'd felt the same ache, even though she didn't have the words to say it. But Gabe knew. She could tell from the way he looked at her that he knew everything that stirred inside her body and her soul.

With that same torturous slow pace, he pressed his hand against her bare stomach. His fingers moved over the lacy panel of her low-cut panties. Leigh arched her back, and hips, to feel more of that touch.

"Say my name, Leigh," he told her, his voice thick. "I want to hear you say my name again."

"Gabe," she obliged. But then almost immediately, she went stiff. "Gabe..."

He must have noticed her reaction because he stopped. "What's wrong?"

She shook her head, already trying to move away from him. "I..."

"Tell me what's wrong."

She pressed her hands on each side of her head. "I remember something."

Only because she was looking at him did she notice the alarm that fired through his eyes. Just like that, the moment and the passion were gone. Those few words were obviously the slap back to reality they both needed.

"Did I try to call you a couple of days ago?" she asked.

He nodded. "You left a message at my apartment in New Orleans. You asked me to meet you at the lake."

Yes. That was it. That was the image that flashed into her head. Her on the phone…somewhere. And she was calling Gabe. "So that's how you knew I'd be there."

Gabe slowly pulled the sides of her robe back in place, stepped away from her and reached for his beer. He finished it off in one quick gulp. "I arrived just in time to see the car speed away. I was about to go after it when I noticed the movement in the water."

And she was that *movement* in the water. "Do you remember if I said anything else in that message?"

"I remember it word for word," he admitted. "You said you had something to tell me. That I should meet you at Lake Pontchartrain on the east end of the old Slidell Bridge so we wouldn't be seen. It's been closed to traffic for years. You added that if something should go wrong then I was to get to Philip in Houston."

"Philip in Houston," she repeated. Yes. That sounded right.

At first.

But then the prickle started up the back of her neck. The feeling that went through her made her feel on the verge of a panic attack. Something was wrong. Terribly wrong. ''We have to get to Houston, Gabe.''

He nodded and closed the window over the sink. ''And we will, right after we've spoken to Frank.''

Because her legs suddenly seemed wobbly, she sat down at the table. It didn't help. The panic attack seemed so close to the surface that she didn't know if she could control it. ''There's something...about Houston.'' But what? Leigh tried to force herself to remember. ''I think my brother might be in danger. All I know is that I *have* to get back to Houston right away.''

Gabe sat down across from her and reached for her hand. Unlike his previous touch, there was nothing carnal about this. He obviously saw how close she was to losing it and wanted to comfort her.

''Listen, Leigh, if Jinx hasn't been able to find Philip, no one can. That means he's safe. If Frank can tell us who Dayton's accomplice is, then we have something to work with. We can get this person off our backs, and neither you nor your brother will be in danger.''

Maybe. And maybe not. Still, Gabe was right about one thing. They did need to find out what Frank knew. It wouldn't do any good for them to go racing to Houston when she had no idea where in Houston even to look for her brother.

She pulled her hand from his and pressed her fingertips, hard, to her temples. ''God, I hate this amnesia. There's something I'm supposed to be doing.

Something important. I just know it. I *feel* it. And I don't have a clue what it is."

"It'll come to you. Beating yourself up won't help." He stood and pushed the chair back under the table. "Why don't you go to bed? You might remember something else after a good night's sleep."

Leigh didn't think she'd be doing much sleeping, but she did need to try. With a midnight rendezvous with Frank, it might be days before she got another chance to rest.

"You can sleep in Maria's old room," Gabe said, helping her from the chair. "It's at the end of the hall. I've already locked up, and I turned on the security alarm. It's not state-of-the-art, but it'll give us enough warning just in case."

Just in case those gunmen returned. With the other things that had gone on, Leigh had almost forgotten about them.

She retrieved her gun from the table and stepped out into the hallway. "Where will you be?" she asked.

"I'll take the couch."

So he would be close to the front door, no doubt. In other words, he'd spend the night standing guard. "Let me know if you need some relief."

A short burst of air rushed out of his mouth. It was almost a smothered laugh. Leigh nearly laughed herself. That wasn't the best choice of words considering what had just happened between them. "I meant if you needed me to take a turn standing guard."

"Yeah." He paused. "I know what you meant."

No doubt. But knowing it didn't do anything to lessen the strain she felt between them.

She motioned toward the kitchen. "I'm sorry about what just happened, Gabe." It was paltry at best. But it was the only thing she could offer him at the moment. "I would say it won't happen again, but I'll save my breath."

"Good idea." He turned and walked into the living room.

She stood there and watched while he sank onto the sturdy, floral sofa. There was probably something else she should say to him. Perhaps a confession that she no longer doubted that they'd once been in love. But that would probably only make things worse.

It would for her anyway.

Leigh didn't need any verbal reminders as to how deep her feelings for Gabe once were. Nor did she need to dwell on the fact that once her memory returned, she just might realize those feelings, that love, was still there.

# *Chapter Ten*

Leigh lifted her head from against the window when Gabe drove past the sign that announced the Grand Valley city limits. Finally, they'd reached their destination. They had taken what seemed to be the most roundabout route to get there, with Gabe meandering down one back road after another.

"Do you have any idea where this place is that we're supposed to meet Frank?" she asked, glancing around the pristine houses and shops that dotted the landscape. It wasn't a large town, but it seemed spread out.

"The house is on Outrider Street."

Since he didn't check a map or even look at the road signs, she figured Gabe had been there before. But then, it was an FBI safe house. She, too, might have visited it when she was still on the Evidence Response Team.

She glanced at the clock on the dash. It was still nearly a half hour until midnight. Not a vast amount of time, but they'd already spent the entire day just killing time.

And trying to ignore each other.

Gabe had been far more successful at it than she had.

Basically, he'd just clammed up. When he did speak to answer one of her chitchat-type questions, he kept his answers to a bare minimum. In the five hours it'd taken them to get from his childhood home to Grand Valley, Gabe had really only passed on a few bits and pieces of new information. Leigh now knew that she was twenty-nine and, other than sugary coffee, she had a fondness for old Bogart movies, chocolate ice cream and reading murder mysteries. Not exactly a storehouse of information.

What he carefully avoided was any discussion about what had gone on the night before in the kitchen. Or any comment about their past relationship.

It was just as well. She had no idea what to say to him about those things either. It was clear that Gabe wasn't eager to resume a relationship with her, but he'd certainly had trouble resisting anything physical.

But then, so had she.

When Gabe slowed down the car, Leigh followed his gaze to the two-story house on Outrider Street. "That's it?" It looked like the dozen or so other houses that lined both sides of the street. Nondescript. A cookie-cutter image of the other houses around it. And that was probably why the FBI had chosen it.

Gabe nodded and drove right past it. He parked at the end of the block in front of a small park.

"Do you think Frank's already in there?" Leigh glanced out the back window. She could easily see the house, but there weren't any lights on inside.

"Maybe."

But since he settled against the seat, that obviously meant he didn't intend to go in early. Maybe because it might scare off Frank, and maybe because he wanted to give Jinx a little more time to arrive.

"So, what's the plan?" she asked.

Gabe made himself more comfortable, stretching out his arm so that it rested on the back of her seat. It wasn't necessarily intentional. There wasn't much room in the two-seater car, and his arms were long.

"We wait, and when it's time, I walk to the house and go inside."

"That's it? It sounds too risky. What if someone used Frank to set a trap for us?"

"Well, I obviously won't knock on the door and wait for someone to invite me in. I'll go around back and get in without being seen."

Leigh didn't like that any better than the other part. "And what if Frank accidentally shoots you because he thinks you're someone else?"

Gabe lay back on the headrest. "He's expecting me. Besides, no one else is supposed to be here."

"You don't know that for sure. Jinx knows we'll be here. He could have told someone."

He angled his eyes in her direction. "We've been

through this. Jinx is a decent guy. I've known him for years.''

That didn't mean she would trust him. Leigh tried a different approach. ''What if the accomplice is waiting inside?''

Gabe shrugged. ''It won't change what I have to do. One way or another, I have to meet Frank. I'll disarm the security system and hope for the best.''

''Great day, this sounds like no plan at all. All right, Gabe, answer this one. After we get in and disarm the system, then what? Do we just pray that no one blows us away?''

He leaned closer and cupped her chin. ''Let's get one thing straight right now. There's no *we* to this plan. *You* will wait here in the car while *I* go inside. I have no intention of taking you into that house.''

This wasn't at all the way she thought things would be, and Leigh was sure her expression showed it. ''But you're going in,'' she pointed out.

''Because I don't have a choice. I want to get in and out as fast as possible. I can't do that if I have to worry about you, too.''

Was he right? Leigh had to concede that he might be. Frank possibly held information that could save their lives.

Or get them killed.

Either way, they had to know. And either way with the stitches in her ankle, she would be a liability to Gabe.

She huffed, frustrated at the conclusion she'd come to. "Why do you get to come up with the plans?"

"Because I don't have amnesia. When you get your memory back, you can come up with all the plans you want." He glanced at her foot. "How's the ankle holding up?"

"Fine."

He took two painkillers from the first-aid kit and handed her a bottle of water. "These might help."

She took the tablets, wishing there were such an easy solution to the rest of her problems. "When we're done here, will we leave straight for Houston?"

"That depends. If Frank tells us what we want to know, then yes. But before we go driving all over Houston, I'm hoping Jinx will come up with an address for Philip."

Leigh hoped the same thing. There were too many hitches in her life right now—her brother's whereabouts and safety were just part of them. She could add Houston to that list. Just the mention of the place sent her blood pressure climbing. And then there was Gabe. When they'd worked through all those other problems, she would still have to figure out what to do about him.

The physical attraction was still there. The incident at the house had proven that. The heat still crackled between them even now. That meant whatever had happened to drive them apart, it hadn't destroyed the feelings they had for each other. Well, not all of them anyway. However, it had put a wedge between them that seemed to dissolve with each smoldering glance they shared.

If it'd just been those glances, Leigh could have dealt with it better. But it was much more than that. Gabe was someone she trusted. She no longer doubted that. That phone call she remembered making was one of the most important calls of her life, and she'd phoned the one man who could save her and her brother. She wouldn't have made that call to just anyone.

"You're sure quiet over there," Gabe said to her. "Are you thinking I owe you an apology for what went on back at the house?"

She nearly choked on the drink of water she'd just taken. "No apology. I was a willing participant."

Incredibly willing.

Leigh had already opened her mouth to delve into that can of worms he'd just opened, but Gabe spoke before she could. "It's time to go," he said softly. "I want to go over the rules."

"Rules?" she repeated. He'd made it sounds as if they were back in elementary school. "Why do you get to come up with the rules?"

"They're like plans—my territory." He didn't even pause after that glib remark. "Keep your gun ready and stay put. I mean, don't move an inch. If and only if I signal do you come into that house."

"What's the signal?"

"I'll flicker the lights."

She felt her eyes widen. "And how will you manage that if someone's holding a gun on you?"

"*Mi vida,* the only time I'll flicker those lights is when and if the place is safe."

"So, I'm not supposed to come to your aid even if I can save your life?" Leigh asked.

"That's right. But don't worry, I'll be fine." He put his hand on the door handle, but he didn't open it. He hesitated a moment. Then, two. "By the way, if something does happen, Jinx will find you. He'll take you someplace safe."

That sent her stomach into a tailspin. "But you just said you'd be fine."

She would have added more, much more, if he hadn't kissed her. It happened so fast that Leigh didn't even see it coming. It didn't last long. Hardly more than a taste. He broke the contact and stared into her eyes. She was pretty sure she no longer looked argumentative.

"You said that complicates things," she pointed out. And it did. Big time. She couldn't think her way out of a paper bag when Gabe kissed her.

"I know. What can I say—I'm weak. And I've gotta go."

With that calmly uttered remark, Gabe got out of the car and started toward the house. She kept her gaze on him, watching until he disappeared into the darkness.

Her fears certainly didn't disappear.

If something happened to Gabe... But Leigh

couldn't even finish that thought. Instead, she forced herself to concentrate on something she could control—a backup plan of her own. If Gabe hadn't returned within fifteen minutes, she would say to heck with his rules. She'd go in after him. After all, those kind of rules were made to be broken.

The minutes crawled by.

She kept a close watch on the house, praying that everything was all right. But she saw nothing. No flickering lights. No shadows. No sign of life. It made the muscles in her chest tighten even more.

God, how many times had she sat through something like this? She didn't have a specific answer, but Leigh knew this wasn't a first. No, there'd been other cases, other assignments where she'd been in a position like this. Odd though, the potential danger didn't frighten her nearly as much as the thought of Gabe going in that house alone.

At the end of her self-imposed time limit, Leigh got out of the car, taking the gun with her. She didn't know exactly what she intended to do, but if she could get closer to the house, she might catch a glimpse of Gabe. That glimpse would hopefully be enough to reassure her that he was all right.

She walked toward the house, trying to stay focused on her surroundings. She didn't want another gunman sneaking up on her like the one at the clinic. Nor did she want a neighbor to see her skulking around and call the cops. A squad car with flashing lights wouldn't please Gabe or Frank.

Everything suddenly seemed quiet. Too quiet. And her instincts screamed that something wasn't right. Instead of staying on the sidewalk where she could easily be seen, Leigh went in the same direction Gabe had taken. She cut across one of the postage-stamp lawns and into a narrow greenbelt. Shrubs and mature trees dotted the area, providing her with an adequate hiding space.

She hoped.

A dog barked, and because it sounded nearby, Leigh froze. She hadn't thought her heart could race any faster, but it did. Was is possible she had a fear of dogs? Well, it didn't matter. This was no time to be neurotic. She had to make sure Gabe was all right.

She reached the house and flattened her body against the side so she could peek into the kitchen window. The only light came from the dim bulb over the stove, but it was enough to see things she didn't want to see.

Some kind of struggle had obviously taken place. A violent struggle. Broken dishes littered the counter. Chairs were knocked helter-skelter. What looked to be a bloody handprint was on the doorway leading into the hall. There was no sign of anyone, either wounded or otherwise.

"Please don't let that be Gabe's blood," she whispered to herself. But just the sight of it caused her breath to stall in her throat.

Speeding up her search, Leigh slipped around the corner and climbed onto the back porch that spanned the entire width of the house. The overhead light was out. Whether by design or chance, it didn't matter. The darkness cloaked her, and she hoped that was an advantage.

The darkness, however, didn't make it easy for her to move around. Groping blindly, she caught onto the arm of the porch swing and used it to maneuver her way to the door. A door that she prayed wasn't locked. Unlike Gabe, she didn't think she had any lock-picking skills. At least not skills that she remembered anyway.

It was obviously too late to consider something so critical, but it occurred to her that she might have breached some sort of perimeter security if Gabe hadn't disarmed it. Leigh didn't want to think about how quickly and how aggressively someone would respond to a triggered security system at an FBI safe house. It would no doubt be more than just squad cars with flashing lights. And maybe that wouldn't be such a bad thing.

After all, things didn't look secure by a long shot.

Leigh heard a sound come from inside the house—something like a swish, as if someone had blown out a candle. A shot fired from a silencer, maybe?

Oh, God.

If it had been a shot, then the struggle was still going on, and Gabe was probably right in the middle of it. Since he didn't have a silencer on his gun, that meant someone was shooting at him. Or at Frank. Either way, it wasn't good.

She forced herself to get moving and immediately tripped over something. Struggling to hang on to her gun and to break her fall, Leigh didn't have time to see what had snagged her foot. That is, she didn't see it until she hit the porch and came face-to-face with it.

The obstacle was a man.

He was on his stomach, unmoving, his face turned to the side. His eyes were blank. Lifeless.

Dead.

Choking back a scream, Leigh frantically searched that face to see if it was familiar. It wasn't Gabe. Thank God, it wasn't Gabe.

She scrambled away from the body, keeping her gun raised in case she had to defend herself. She bolted forward only to run head-on into something else.

Not something.

Someone.

Solid, strong arms suddenly clamped around her. A hand closed over her mouth before she could even call out for help.

And she was trapped.

# *Chapter Eleven*

Gabe barely dodged the elbow that Leigh tried to ram into his stomach. He wasn't quite so successful avoiding the kick to his shin. Or the Muay Thai boxing move she used after that. She was in a fight-or-flight mode and had obviously chosen to fight. Too bad he was the one she was fighting.

"It's me," Gabe managed.

Leigh continued to struggle. She pivoted, and went after him again, but he managed to get a tight lock on her. It took several seconds for her mind to register what her eyes had already seen.

"It's all right," he said directly against her ear.

No, it wasn't all right, but it was the best he could offer her in the hopes it would settle her down. Her nerves were in a million pieces. Her body, a snarl of adrenaline, fear and relief. Gabe understood every single one of those emotions because he was feeling them himself.

"Gabe," she said as if just realizing who he was.

She latched onto him and buried her face against his neck. "You're not hurt. Thank God."

"No." He wouldn't let himself be even remotely pleased with Leigh's concern for him. Nor would he let himself be too angry that she'd followed him to the house. Even with the stern warning he'd given her, he figured she would come after him.

"But that man—"

"He was dead when I got here." Gabe eased her around so she wouldn't be tempted to glance at the body. And so they wouldn't be seen by anyone who just happened to look out a window. He moved Leigh deep into the shadows of the porch.

With her breath racing, she pulled slightly away and met his gaze. When she spoke, there was some grit back in her voice. "And you went inside anyway?"

"I had to. I had to find out what was going on."

She shook her head as if trying to understand that. "Is it Frank?"

"No. I don't know who it is. Someone unlucky, that's for sure. I think Frank's still inside."

Her eyes widened. "You saw him?"

"I heard him," Gabe corrected. "At least I think it was Frank. Someone rigged one of the bedroom doors with an explosive device. I heard someone or something inside, maybe even a fired shot. But if I open the door, the whole place will probably go up."

"Sweet heaven." She pressed her fingertips to her mouth for a moment. The alarm, however, didn't stay in her eyes long. Her FBI training apparently kicked in, and Gabe could see she was trying to work things out. ''What about going through the window?''

''There are metal bars. Security measures put in by the Bureau. I don't think we'll get through those without a key, and the key doesn't seem to be anywhere inside. My guess is the person who set those explosives made sure we wouldn't have an easy way to get into that room.''

''Maybe Jinx is around here somewhere and has the key?'' Leigh suggested.

Gabe shook his head. ''I haven't seen him.'' Nor would he since he'd told Jinx to stay out of sight. Besides, he was positive that Jinx wouldn't have the key. It should have been in the safe, which meant someone had taken it.

''I was about to shoot a hole through one of the walls to try to get to Frank,'' he explained, keeping his voice in a whisper. ''But then I heard you out here and thought someone was breaking into the place.''

Leigh took a step toward the door. ''Then let's go inside. I'll help you shoot through the wall.''

He stopped her from taking a second step. Gabe caught onto her shoulder and held on tight. ''I don't plan to start shooting at anything until I take you back to the car.''

''The car is the last place I want to be.'' She gave a frustrated huff and mumbled something under her breath. ''Gabe, I'll be in danger no matter where I am. At least if I'm with you, we can watch out for each other.''

He gave that some thought. It sounded right, until he remembered the *least* safe place was inside the house. Well, maybe. Maybe there was no such thing as a safe place with Dayton's accomplice running around loose. A bullet was a bullet no matter where it was fired.

Gabe dodged her gaze and tipped his eyes upward to seek divine guidance. Or at least to get a grip on some common sense. Unfortunately, he didn't get either. "I'm positive I'll regret this," he heard himself say.

"Maybe. But if so, we'll regret it together." She raised her weapon. "Let's go."

Cursing himself and the mess they were in, he opened the door and stepped back into the kitchen. "Watch our backs," he reminded her. "I'll take care of anything else."

He led her through the L-shaped room, stepping around the overturned chairs and debris. "I wasn't in here when this happened," he let her know when he heard her start to mumble again.

"Thank God. Whose blood is that?"

Gabe glanced at the handprint on the wall before they went into the living room. "I don't know. Maybe the guy on the porch. Frank might have managed to get off a few shots before someone put him in that room."

"But why wouldn't they just kill Frank? Why go through all the trouble to rig that door so it would blow up?"

He didn't have time to answer her. The noise stopped him cold. There was a crash at the far end of the room. The glass exploded, the shards flying through the air toward them. Somehow, Gabe managed to haul her behind him.

And then he saw it.

A fist-size gunmetal-colored canister landed on the floor.

"Get out of here!" he yelled.

With hardly more than a glance at the canister bomb that was only a few yards from them, Gabe shoved her back into the hallway that led to the kitchen.

"What is that thing?" she asked. "God, is it a bomb?"

He grabbed Leigh and tried to get her to safety. He wasn't fast enough. They'd barely made it to the entryway of the kitchen when the deafening blast tore through the living room and the hallway.

The impact knocked Leigh to the floor, and Gabe followed on top of her with his body. Fragments of the canister flew through the air and pelted against the walls and ceiling. He thought of Frank trapped in that room. But there was no way Gabe could get to him. The place suddenly looked like a war zone, and his first instinct was to protect Leigh.

When the fragments stopped raining down on them, Gabe rolled off her. In the same motion, he forced her to her feet and got them moving into the kitchen. They'd hardly had time to take a step when there was another crash through the other window in the dining room. He heard a second canister land on the floor.

He pushed Leigh on the other side of the refrigerator, praying it would be enough to protect them. Gabe braced himself for the next blast.

He didn't have to wait long.

Like the first, the impact shook the house, and debris and glass shot everywhere. A chunk of ceiling just above their heads gave way. It would have crashed on them if they hadn't scrambled across the floor toward the back door.

Gabe forced himself to put a chokehold on his rage, but it took every ounce of his self-control.

Damn the person responsible for this.

Damn his twisted, evil mind.

And while Gabe was doling out damns, he added a harsh one for himself. He'd been a damn fool to allow Leigh to get anywhere near this house. To *this.* In doing so, he'd underestimated his opponent's capabilities, and it had almost gotten her killed.

That wouldn't happen again.

Knowing he had to get them out of the house before it collapsed around them, Gabe pushed Leigh toward the back door. Even in the dark, dust-filled room, he could see that her face was the color of skim milk. She wasn't just scared. She was terrified.

With reason.

Even if they made it out of the house, there was no guarantee that the person who'd fired those canisters wouldn't be waiting for them.

He knew that.

Apparently, so did she.

Unfortunately, it was a chance he had to take.

He shoved open the door and maneuvered himself onto the back porch just ahead of her. There was another crash of wood, metal and glass. Then another.

Gabe didn't wait around. ''Run!'' he ordered. He grabbed her arm and pulled her onto the back porch.

Probably because he didn't give her a choice, Leigh kept up with his pace down the steps and across the yard. Like Gabe, she kept her gun raised. And ready. He prayed it would be enough if someone fired at them.

''Where to?'' she asked.

Gabe couldn't answer—he kept them running. Behind them, a vicious blast ripped through the house. The glass left in the windows burst outward, sending flames and jagged shards right out at them. The house exploded into a fireball. Black coils of smoke rose, smearing into the night sky.

Hell. If Frank was in that house, then he was a dead man.

''Keep running, Leigh!'' Gabe shouted.

He caught a glimpse of the shadowy figure then. And the gun. It was drawn and ready to fire. Gabe pulled up quickly, trying to stop their forward motion, but he couldn't.

It was too late.

# *Chapter Twelve*

Gabe must have seen the gun and the shadowy figure at the same moment Leigh did. He tried to step in front of her, but she wanted no part of that. He'd already risked his life too many times to save her.

He swerved toward the approaching gunman, and Leigh pulled up by his side, aiming her weapon as well. But it wasn't exactly the threat her body had braced itself for. Well, maybe it wasn't. It was Jinx, and he was making his way across the yard straight toward them.

Leigh didn't lower her gun even though Gabe did.

''Are you all right?'' Jinx shouted over the noise of the fire and falling debris.

''What do you think? Someone just tried to kill us,'' Leigh icily informed him. And for all she knew, Jinx could have been the one to do it. Of course, she knew he was supposed to be somewhere in the area—Gabe had told her that. But that didn't give Leigh any reassurance.

Gabe caught onto her arm again. "We can't stay out here in the open."

He was right. With the men on each side of her, they began to run again. Where, she didn't know. Gabe didn't head in the direction of the car, which was just as well. It probably wasn't safe to go there.

"Did you see who fired those explosives?" Gabe asked Jinx. He stopped just behind a row of tall hedges near the street and looked around.

"No, but I think it must have come from one of those trees." He pointed to a cluster of towering oaks in the park area where they'd left the car.

Gabe glanced in that direction. "Yeah. The person probably climbed a tree and used some kind of modified artillery tube to deliver the canisters."

If so, that meant Jinx wouldn't have had time to fire them and then climb back down to run to the house. But Leigh wasn't about to buy that tree-climbing scenario. A modified artillery tube could be fired from anywhere, including the front lawn.

Gabe turned her toward him. "I need to get you out of here while I try to find out if Frank is still alive."

She was already shaking her head before he finished. "I'd rather stay with you."

"I can't—"

The sudden movement at the end of the row of hedges cut him off. All three shifted toward the person who rounded the corner.

"Mind telling me what the devil all of you are doing here?" Teresa Walters snarled. The woman looked harried. Not at all like the composed agent she'd seemed back at the clinic. Teresa gulped in her breath as if she'd just run a long distance.

''I might ask you the same thing,'' Gabe calmly remarked. ''Did you just happened to be in the neighborhood?''

Teresa fired a tight glance at Jinx before she answered. ''No, I was looking for you.''

''Well, you obviously found us,'' Leigh confirmed. ''I don't suppose you know who just tried to kill us?''

The other woman shook her head. ''No. I didn't see anything or anybody.''

If Gabe had any doubts if that was the truth, he didn't voice them. He tipped his head toward what remained of the house. ''Frank Templeton might be dead in there. There's another body on the back porch, and you didn't see a thing. That's not a good endorsement for your skills of observation.''

''I just arrived a few minutes ago,'' Teresa quickly assured him, obviously not bothering to address his sarcasm. ''Now, perhaps you'd tell me how long you've been here and what happened?''

The sarcasm stayed in Gabe's voice. ''Funny you should ask that. Leigh, Jinx and I arrived just a couple of minutes ago, too. No one answered the door, so we went inside to have a look around, and that's when someone started to shoot canister bombs at us. We were just about to call you and report it.''

Teresa didn't look as if she bought that fish story

at all. ''Tell me what's going on, Gabe. Who's responsible for this?''

''I was hoping you could tell me,'' he answered. ''Frank called and asked me to meet him.''

''You actually saw him?'' Teresa volleyed glances between Gabe and the house.

''No, but he asked me to meet him at midnight.''

Leigh didn't want to put off the most obvious question any longer. ''So why'd you come, Agent Walters?''

She didn't even hesitate. ''The ATF had the place under surveillance, and when you showed up, they called me because I told them I wanted to talk to you. I got here as fast as I could.''

Gabe took up where Leigh had left off. ''And you just happened to be in Grand Valley, Texas?''

''No. I accessed your messages and heard the one Frank left on your machine in your apartment in New Orleans.''

''But I erased that message,'' Gabe informed her.

Teresa shrugged. ''There are ways, as you well know.''

''Ways,'' Gabe repeated. ''I guess you had to come up with plan B when I found that transmitter you'd planted in Leigh's bandage.''

Leigh stared at the woman, waiting for her to deny it, but Teresa didn't deny anything. ''That was my insurance that I'd be able to find you if you didn't follow orders. And I don't think I need to point out that I was right.'' She pulled out her phone. ''Why didn't you and Leigh make your way to a safe house earlier?''

''But we did,'' Leigh said with sappy innocence. ''We're standing in front of one now.''

Again, Teresa didn't seem to react to that except to check her watch and take a surreptitious glance around the street where neighbors were starting to gather to watch the blaze. In the distance, Leigh could hear approaching sirens. Obviously, someone had alerted the local authorities. That didn't surprise her. Those explosions had jarred the entire neighborhood.

''I never thought you'd do something this stupid,'' Teresa mumbled. ''You shouldn't have run from me.''

''Well, someone didn't do a great job of providing security at the clinic, did they?'' Leigh pointed out. ''We had to fight our way past four gunmen and barely made it out of there alive.''

''That was still no reason to stay on the run. Security failed,'' Teresa stated firmly, ''and now we're trying to figure out why. We'll have answers soon.''

''Forgive me if I don't hold my breath waiting for that to happen,'' Leigh retorted.

Teresa stared at her a moment. ''We're on the same side, Leigh. Don't forget that.''

''Are we actually on the same side? Because the lines are a little fuzzy here. Somebody is killing people and trying to kill others, namely Gabe and me, and all of that's happened while you and I are on the same flipping side. Makes me wonder if I'd be better off ending this association right now.''

"You can't just *end* it," Teresa snapped. "You need protection, and I'm assigned to give it to you."

Leigh groaned. "I'd rather have a BB gun and a Boy Scout. I'd stand a better chance of making it out of this alive." She couldn't be sure, but she thought she heard Gabe try to muffle a laugh.

"You stand a better chance if you let me do my job."

"Once again, we don't agree. The only person I'm going to trust is Gabe. Got that? So you can just peddle your services somewhere else, Agent Walters. If you really want something to occupy your time, why don't you find out if Frank Templeton's body is inside that house?"

"I need to make a few calls," Gabe announced before Teresa could say if she would act on Leigh's suggestion. "And I need to get a closer look at the house."

Leigh was about to tell him that wasn't a good idea, but the look he gave her had her rethinking that. He obviously had something in mind and wanted her to play along.

"I won't be long," Gabe assured her. He pulled her aside and whispered the rest of what he had to say. "There's a silver car parked at the end of the street. Go there in a couple of minutes." He must have seen the look of uncertainty that went through her eyes because he gave her hand a gentle squeeze. "It's all right. I'll cover you until you're safe inside."

Leigh didn't like the idea of being left alone with

Teresa, but then she could have said the same thing about making her way to that car. She just hoped that Gabe knew what he was doing.

When the men walked away, Teresa rifled through her purse and came up with a cigarette. She didn't light it but instead ran her fingers over it as if trying to decide if she really wanted to smoke it. "Gabe told me your memory was coming back," Teresa stated matter-of-factly. "Any truth to that?"

Gabe had said that to shake things up a little. It meant she, too, should stick to that story.

"I don't remember everything," Leigh answered. "But some key things have come back." Key things, if she counted the phone call to Gabe and the image of him naked. Pretty sparse pickings as far as memories went, but Leigh kept that part to herself.

"I suppose Gabe told you about all the problems you two were having before you disappeared?" Teresa asked.

Leigh looked back at Gabe. He was standing to the side of the house, his phone pressed to his ear. Jinx was making a call of his own. "Yes. We were talking about a divorce."

Teresa made a slight sound in her throat. "And do you know why?"

Leigh didn't think she cared much for the direction of this conversation. "Yes, I know. He made a mistake and put his trust in the wrong person, namely, Joe Dayton."

"Gabe told you that?" Teresa gave a heavy sigh

and pushed back a wisp of hair that had slipped from her French twist. "He wasn't supposed to. He never sticks with the plan."

"I'm not absolutely sure, but I think I like that about him." Leigh added a dry grin because she knew it would rile the other woman.

Teresa snapped the cigarette in half and tossed it on the ground. "You're falling for him all over again, aren't you?"

Leigh stared at the cigarette for several seconds before she eased her gaze to Teresa. "Now, just why would that concern you?"

"Because I'd like to think we're friends."

Friends? Leigh didn't need her memory to know that wasn't true. "And why would you think that?"

"Well, I've known you for a long time now. We've even worked on some cases together."

"And this is leading..." Leigh gestured with her hand. "Where exactly?"

"Well, since you can't remember everything, I think it's only fair to warn you that Gabe hasn't always acted in your best interest. There were times when your marriage was rocky at best."

"Yes, I know. I'm still waiting for you to tell me where this is leading."

"It's not leading anywhere. I'm just trying..." But Teresa stopped and shook her head as if she shouldn't say anything else.

"Obviously. I think the term you're looking for, Teresa, is 'causing trouble.' You can save it. I already have more trouble than I can handle.'' Leigh turned and walked away.

She had no idea that Gabe had stepped up behind her until she heard his voice. ''Anything wrong?'' he asked.

''We have to talk,'' Leigh said softly. ''But it can wait.''

She saw an expression on Gabe's face that she had yet to encounter. Not quite anger but something close. Fury, perhaps. It actually frightened her, and she hoped this particular emotion wasn't aimed at her.

Gabe drew her away from Teresa. ''There's been a slight change of plans. I just talked to Jinx, and we're getting the hell out of here, understand?''

She hesitated before giving a slow nod. ''All right. Any idea how we're going to do that? I don't think Teresa will just let us leave without causing a fuss.''

''Jinx will tell her to back off. Maybe this time she'll actually listen to him.'' He tipped his head to the silver-colored car parked at the end of the street. ''That's where we're headed. Stay behind me.''

Leigh nodded, but before she could take even a step, Gabe caught onto her arm. ''Do you still trust me?'' he asked.

She almost gave him a flippant comeback, but that tormented look in his eyes stopped her. Whatever was going on inside his head, it wasn't pleasant, and she thought its cause was more than what had just happened with the blast and the dead man.

''I trust you, Gabe.'' And she came up on her tiptoes and brushed a kiss on his cheek. To reassure him maybe, and maybe because she knew Teresa would see it. The kiss didn't stay on his cheek, however. Nor did it stay gentle and reassuring. With his breath coming out in rapid hot bursts, he gripped the back of her neck and captured her mouth in a searing kiss.

"Is there something else I should know about?" Leigh asked when he finally broke away from her. She couldn't imagine the situation being worse, but it was obvious that something had upset Gabe.

"We'll talk later."

That didn't do a thing to reassure her. God, what else had gone wrong?

"Wait a minute," Teresa barked when she saw them start to walk away. She covered the mouthpiece of her phone with her hand. "Just where do you think you're going?"

"It's all right, Teresa," Jinx called out. He came back across the yard toward her. Leigh didn't have to know specifically what Jinx was saying, but it was obvious that the woman was about to receive a dressing-down.

Gabe didn't waste any time. He led Leigh straight to the car, unlocking the vehicle with the remote on a key chain that he pulled from his pocket.

"Get in the back seat," he instructed. "And stay down. We'll leave just as soon as Jinx gets here."

She crouched on the floor but peered at Gabe over the seat. "Jinx?"

"He's coming with us."

Leigh didn't know how to react to that. She certainly didn't want the man tagging along, but maybe Gabe needed him for something. Still, she didn't plan to let down her guard anytime soon.

"What the hell?" Gabe mumbled. With his gaze fixed on the passenger's window, he turned his weapon in that direction. "There's Frank Templeton."

Leigh popped up from her hiding space and saw him coming directly toward them. "He made it out of the house. I can't believe it."

The tall, red-haired man was hunched over and literally skulking his way around the other cars. To say he looked beleaguered was putting it mildly. His clothes were torn and dirty, and his hair tangled wildly around his face.

Gabe pushed the button to lower the window a fraction but didn't open the door. Leigh also noticed that he kept his hand on his gun. Not surprising. She wasn't in the frame of mind to trust anyone either. For all she knew, Frank could be the one behind this. He'd certainly had as much opportunity and motive as anyone else.

"Leigh," Frank said on a rise of breath. "Gabe found you. Thank God."

"Yes. Are you all right?"

"Not really. I was waiting in the house for Gabe, but someone tried to kill me."

"Yeah, I know. They tried to do the same thing to Gabe and me." She glanced around to make sure no one else was coming their way. "Listen, Frank, I don't have a lot of time to explain this, but I have amnesia, and I don't know what's going on."

He gave her a puzzled look, but that look soon turned to something more—alarm. "Neither do I, Leigh. That's why I wanted to talk to Gabe and you."

She shook her head, not understanding what he meant. "But why did you disappear if you didn't know what was going on?"

"For the same reason you did. It didn't take a genius to figure out that Dayton wanted us both dead."

"Dayton killed himself two years ago," Gabe reminded him.

"Yes, but he wasn't working alone. I knew Joe couldn't put together an operation like that on his own. Great day, we're talking three tons of weapons. Maybe more. It would have taken him years to siphon off that much without someone noticing."

Leigh had no idea the volume of weapons was that high. No wonder Gabe had figured the bulk of them hadn't been moved. Plus, they were hot goods. Probably every law enforcement agency would be looking for a cache like that. But in two years, only a few had surfaced.

Why?

An accomplice would have known the location of that storage facility. Well, maybe. Maybe Dayton hadn't trusted his partner with that kind of information. So, that meant Frank and she were possibly the only two people who even had a clue as to the cache's location.

And that made Frank a suspect.

Realizing that she very well could be looking at Dayton's accomplice after-the-fact, she wondered if she should just have Gabe arrest him on the spot. However, Frank was looking at her as if to decide the same thing.

"It's not me," Frank said firmly. "I had nothing to do with Dayton's plan. I didn't even see what was on that disk before it destroyed itself. Can you look me in the eye, Leigh, and say the same thing?"

"Absolutely."

"But how do you know?" he challenged. "You have amnesia."

"I don't need my memory to know that I'm not a criminal. If I'd seen something on that disk, I wouldn't have kept it a secret."

Frank kept his narrowed gaze on her as if trying to decide if he believed her. After a moment, he nodded. "Then someone else is out there. Someone who knows everything."

"Yes, and that person thinks we know the location of the weapons. He or she is willing to kill us to keep a secret. That's why it's important that you stay with us."

"I can't." His gaze cut to Gabe. "You need to get her out of here now."

"That was my plan. Jinx should be here any second. How about you? Where are you headed?"

"Someplace safe."

"Need a ride?" Gabe opened the door then, but it

was more than just a friendly gesture. Gabe's body language and his raised gun made it seem more like an order. "We still have a few things to discuss."

Frank glanced at the drawn weapon and the still-blazing house. "I'll call you to set up another meeting. Someplace private. It's too dangerous for us to talk here." He started to move away.

"Wait," Gabe said in a stern whisper. "How can I reach you?"

"Don't know yet. I'm still looking for the accomplice, and I'm getting very close. Also, don't trust Teresa. There's something not right there." He raised his hand in a hasty farewell and disappeared into some shrubs.

"Shouldn't you go after him?" Leigh asked frantically.

"No. I won't leave you alone."

"But Frank might be able to tell us something."

"You heard what he said, Leigh. He doesn't know who did this. We'll just have to wait for his call. Besides, we're leaving."

Leigh craned her neck so she could look in the rearview mirror. It was Jinx. And from the look on his face, he was not a happy man.

Gabe climbed into the back seat with her, and Jinx got behind the wheel. "Let's get the hell out of here," Jinx insisted. "Now!"

# *Chapter Thirteen*

Gabe glanced behind him. Since Teresa wasn't in hot pursuit, he guessed she was still tied up with the call from the Bureau that Jinx had arranged. That call would buy them some time. Hopefully. But they needed to get away from Grand Valley and the safe house if they didn't want to get caught up in a full-scale investigation.

"Are you all right?" Gabe asked Jinx.

"I'm fine. Who was the man I just saw running from the car?"

Gabe met Jinx's gaze in the rearview mirror and gave him a you're-not-going-to-believe-this look. "Frank Templeton."

"Frank?" Jinx repeated. "I thought for certain that his body was somewhere in that burning house. I take it he's alive and well?"

"Alive, for sure," Gabe informed him. "I don't know about the well part. He looked like hell. He said he still doesn't know who's doing this, that we shouldn't trust Teresa, and he'll call me to set up another meeting."

Gabe hadn't needed Frank's advice about trusting Teresa though. He had no plans to trust either Frank or her.

He checked the street behind them again. No sign of Teresa or anyone else. There was traffic, assorted emergency and law enforcement vehicles, but they were all headed toward the house.

Once they were away from the crime scene, he needed to have that talk with Leigh. She knew something was wrong. He could tell that from the side glances she kept tossing his way. Hell. Teresa had probably told her everything.

Jinx had just made it to the edge of town when his phone rang. Gabe was willing to bet it was Teresa, but he soon learned he would have lost that bet.

"Lieutenant Venegos," Jinx said to the caller. "Please tell me you have good news."

Gabe knew the name. Venegos was a Texas Ranger who often worked with the Bureau on high- and low-profile cases.

"Are you really all right?" Leigh whispered to him.

"I'm fine." She probably thought his somber mood had to do with their brush with death, but that was only part of it. "We have to talk," he let her know.

She nodded. Just nodded. That didn't do a lot to put him at ease. Damn Teresa and her big mouth.

"Our friend in the Texas Rangers found Philip about an hour ago," Jinx relayed when he hung up the phone. ''He's safe. For now, anyway. He's using an assumed name—Tyler Wilkins.''

Leigh moved to the edge of the seat. ''My brother's in Houston?''

''No. He's living near San Antonio. Lieutenant Venegos tracked him down at the nightclub where Philip bartends. He didn't let Philip know anyone was looking for him.''

''Did Venegos give you an address?'' Gabe wanted to know.

''Yeah. Philip rented a place in the country, and the lieutenant thought it might be better for you to go there instead of the nightclub. He tried to call Philip's house, but he only got the machine. Some woman named Jenny recorded the message. Hopefully, I'll have more info on her before we get to San Antonio.''

Gabe was sure Jinx would. By now, Venegos was probably tapping into every information source he had to help them. ''Have you already assigned someone to tail Philip?''

Jinx nodded, but the eye contact he made with Gabe told him plenty. If the Texas Rangers could find Philip, the man needed protection. And fast. They had to get to Leigh's brother before someone else did.

Leigh settled back against the seat. ''So now what—we just drive out to his house and surprise him?''

''You two will,'' Jinx answered. ''You can drop me off at the field office in San Antonio so I can cover our tracks. I want to stop this information trail before someone else picks up on it.''

She nodded, obviously understanding the need for that. "How long before we get there?"

"Four hours."

Of course, that wouldn't be a direct route, but Gabe knew it was necessary for them to cover their own tracks as well as Philip's. Fortunately, Jinx was very good at doing that.

Four hours. Soon they'd be able to see Leigh's brother and could hopefully stop anything bad from happening to him. Philip might also know where she'd been for the past two years, or better yet, he might know who was trying to kill her.

Gabe didn't dare hope for things to be wrapped up in a neat little package. If fact, he only hoped that Leigh could somehow forgive him for what had happened two years earlier.

He made another check of the highway before he angled his body toward her. "What did Teresa tell you back there at the house?"

Even in the dark car, he saw Leigh flinch. Maybe that was because of the abruptness of his voice. Or maybe it was because this was the last thing on earth she wanted to discuss with him.

After a couple of moments, she shrugged. "She was being catty, that's all. Did you two have a thing going, because she sounded a little jealous?"

"Tell me what she said," Gabe repeated, enunciating each word.

She cleared her throat and rubbed her index finger over her eyebrow. "Well, she claimed to be my friend and basically told me that you hadn't always acted in my best interest.''

' And? Tell me everything, Leigh.''

The fidgeting stopped, and she met his gaze head-on. ''What is this all about?''

''Tell me what she said to you.''

It seemed Leigh was about to clam up, but she huffed and continued. ''She was just trying to get to me, that's all. Listen, if you had an affair with her—''

''I didn't have an affair with her, and I want to know the rest of what she said.''

''Gabe, this is ridiculous. What do—''

''Damn it, what did she say?''

She pulled back her shoulders. ''About what?'' Her voice rose to his level.

''You know about what. Now quit playing games with me. What the hell did Teresa say about the baby?''

LEIGH FELT as if he'd slapped her. The breath swooshed of her mouth. ''Baby?'' she managed to say. ''What baby?''

But Gabe didn't answer. ''Stop the car,'' he ordered Jinx.

Jinx glanced back at them. ''Do I need to remind you that you're not out of danger?''

''Just stop the car, damn it! I need to talk to Leigh.''

Jinx added some profanity of his own while he pulled onto the shoulder of the road. The moment he stopped, Gabe threw open the door, obviously ready to get out.

"Stay put," Jinx insisted. "But try not to take too long with this little heart-to-heart, will you? It's not a good idea to hang around here."

"What baby?" Leigh repeated the moment Jinx stepped outside and shut the door.

Gabe stared at her a long time before he answered. "*Our* baby."

She was absolutely certain she'd misunderstood him. That's why Leigh repeated those two words to herself. Our baby. Our baby.

"What are you talking about, Gabe?" But she was almost afraid to hear what he had to say. "We have a baby?"

"No." Gabe cursed softly and looked away. "You thought you were pregnant, but it was a false alarm."

She almost asked for an explanation, but Leigh didn't need him to tell her. Images began to race through her head. Images of her standing in the middle of a room in a hospital gown, of her arm bandaged in a sling. Words followed those out-of-focus images. Words that wouldn't have made sense if Gabe hadn't just told her that she'd once thought she was pregnant.

*"You shouldn't be out of bed,"* Gabe had said to her.

Leigh had just stared at him, her eyes filled not with tears but with anger. *"I heard what you said to Jinx. I heard every word. You didn't want me to have a baby."*

*"I just wasn't expecting this. I thought—"*

But Leigh had cut him off and moved into the hallway outside the room. *"I know what you thought. Well, don't worry, Gabe, you got your wish. There isn't a baby. The doctors did a test, and the results were negative."*

"My God, I remember." Leigh leaned her head against the window.

Almost afraid of what she'd see, she glanced at Gabe. He looked at if he'd just had a knife plunged into his heart. "How much do you remember?"

She wasn't even sure she could say it aloud. She took a deep breath. "The conversation we had in the hospital. You must have just found out that I wasn't pregnant."

"You were very upset," he said as if that explained everything. Gabe didn't even look at her. He stared out the other window. "*We* were upset," he added a moment later.

Leigh waited for him to continue—mainly because she didn't have a clue what to say. Or do. This had obviously been a miserable time in their lives. The lowest of low points. Even now, it hurt just to recall those memories.

Gabe pushed his hand through his hair. "I didn't know that you suspected you were pregnant until the day before Dayton tried to kill you. You told Jinx, and then he told me."

She fired a glance at the man standing outside the car, but he had his attention focused on their surroundings. "Jinx?" she repeated. "Why would I tell him something like that before I let you know?"

"He's our friend, Leigh. I guess you thought you could talk to him about it. You asked him to keep it a secret. But he didn't. He came to me because he thought it was something I should know."

So, Jinx had betrayed her. Well, in a way. She hoped that was the only reason she had the feeling she couldn't trust the man.

"You overheard Jinx telling me," Gabe continued a moment later. "I didn't take the news well."

No, he hadn't. And just like the other images and past conversations, Leigh suddenly remembered that, too. "'I can't believe this,'" she repeated. "That's what you said to Jinx. 'I can't believe she'd do this knowing I'm not ready to be a father.'"

Gabe slowly brought his gaze back to her. "I did say that, yes."

"And then it turned out I wasn't pregnant after all." Leigh shuddered. There was one advantage to having amnesia. She was able to see the incident through eyes not clouded with so much emotion. Unlike Gabe. One look at his face and she knew he was experiencing an even greater pain than she was.

"Earlier, you said we'd agreed not to have children?" she asked.

"We'd agreed to disagree."

Oh. Leigh hadn't considered that angle. "And we had agreed to wait," she concluded. "Any particular reason, or do you just not like kids?"

"I like kids. A lot. It's just I've seen enough crime scenes and enough dead bodies to know just how fast life can end."

There was more to it than that. During their entire ordeal of running from gunmen and nearly getting killed, Gabe had shown absolutely no signs of weakness. But he was showing it now. Leigh figured she was getting a glimpse of a vulnerable side of Agent Gabe Sanchez that few people ever saw. It intrigued her. And made her ache.

"When I was eight, someone kidnapped my sister, Emily," he said softly.

"The one in the picture at your parents' house?"

Gabe nodded. "She was only eleven, and we were on our bikes less than a half mile from our house. A car pulled up next to us, and a man reached out and grabbed her." He snapped his fingers. "Just like that, she was gone."

Leigh barely managed to muffle her gasp. "My God. What happened to her?"

He kept his attention focused outside. "They found her body a week later in a dry creek bed. What they didn't find was the man who killed her. Every time you'd talk about wanting a child, all I could think about was losing someone I loved to a monster."

"I see."

And she did. From Gabe's point of view, having a baby would be like playing a game with stakes that were too high. There were tears in her eyes now, but

Leigh hadn't been aware of them until she felt one spill down her cheek.

"I'm sorry about your sister. About Emily. And I understand why you didn't want to risk having a child of your own." She paused to collect her breath. "It's my guess that our disagreement about the pregnancy got all mixed together with what happened with Dayton. The truth is, I was probably as shocked about the possibility of being pregnant as you were. I'd just had a little more time to adjust to it than you had."

He looked at her then, his gaze combing over her face. "Is that what you remember?"

She shook her head. "I don't have to remember the incident to know that I probably didn't give you a fair shake because of all the mental junk I was going through."

For a while they said nothing else. He just looked at her, and Leigh just looked at him. In his eyes, she saw the swirl of emotions that had brought them to this point.

"I'm sorry," she let him know.

Surprised, he glanced at her. "Why are you sorry?"

"For the way everything turned out." She shook her head. "I don't even know if I'm the same person I was two years ago, but I suspect you haven't changed much."

"You're wrong. I've changed a lot."

And not necessarily for the better. She was responsible for that. She'd let the anger and bitterness drive her away from him. It didn't feel good to know that she'd been a quitter at one of the most important things in her entire life.

"I guess what I'm trying to say," she continued, "is that the things that brought us together five years ago are still there in full working order. The feelings. The connection. The people we are when we're together."

Gabe didn't say a word. He just stared at her.

She tried again. "I'm sorry about the argument, Gabe. Sorry that I left without trying to work things out with you. Sorry that I threw away what was no doubt a good thing. And I'm especially sorry that it took me all this time to figure out that I was wrong."

Leigh held her breath, and waited. She didn't have to wait long.

Gabe reached out and pulled her into his arms. Not for a kiss. Or even a hug. He just held her. And that was exactly what she needed from him.

## *Chapter Fourteen*

There wasn't a car in the driveway in front of Philip's house, but there was a huge Doberman sitting on the porch. The dog looked pretty territorial, and since they were about to invade its territory, Gabe hoped it didn't object too much.

"This might be just a weird case of nerves," Leigh said, staring at the porch as well. "But I don't think I like the idea of that dog being there."

"It's not a weird case of nerves," he assured her. "Not exactly anyway. You had a bad experience a couple of years ago. Some Dobermans came after you when you went to a house to interview a witness. You weren't hurt, but it scared you pretty bad."

"So, that explains why my heart feels ready to pound out of my chest. My body obviously remembers a lot of things my mind doesn't."

Gabe read a lot into that statement. Maybe too much. But it seemed pretty evident that Leigh still responded to him at least on a physical level. After the air-clearing they'd had in the car, he thought maybe she might start to respond beyond just the physical.

He wasn't sure how to feel about that. It was a lot to absorb, especially with everything else going on. He'd have to take it minute by minute and see how things progressed.

"We'll have to get past that dog to get inside, I suppose?" she asked.

Oh, yeah. And Gabe didn't think the fellow planned to move anytime soon. He wasn't barking. Yet. But he appeared to be growling. In other words, he was a watchdog, something he was glad Philip had. It might discourage anyone else from trying to get inside. Unfortunately, that left Gabe with one small problem—he had to find some way to get around the dog so they could get in. He didn't want to sit out in the open waiting for Philip to get home.

He parked the car behind an old barn. It was just a precaution, but he didn't want anyone to know they were there.

"I could carry you in," Gabe suggested when he saw Leigh still eyeing the dog.

"No, I can walk." But she thought about it first. And she latched onto her gun when they got out of the car.

Immediately, the dog shot to his feet. His posture was ready for combat, his teeth bared. A whisper-soft, feral growl rumbled from his throat. That put a dent in Leigh's resolve because she darted behind him. Gabe almost laughed. Here, she'd faced down gunman without so much as a whimper, and yet the dog terrified her.

"He'll probably be friendly once he realizes we're not burglars," he remarked as they walked up the steps.

As if to prove Gabe wrong, the dog chose that exact moment to growl. It was more of a perfunctory grumble, but it was enough to send Leigh crashing into him again. "It'll be all right," he murmured to both the dog and Leigh.

He cautiously offered the dog the back of his hand, but the canine didn't move from his position. Not right away. A few moments later, he stooped lower.

"Sit," Gabe firmly told the animal.

Thank God he listened. Within seconds, the canine's jaw relaxed, and he began thumping his tail on the porch.

"See?" Gabe said. "He's friendly."

From the grip Leigh still had on his arm, she probably didn't believe that. "So, how do we get inside? And please don't tell me we have to wait out here until Philip gets home."

He fished into his pocket and brought out the key. "This was under the mat in your rental car, the one with your fingerprints on it."

"And you think it'll fit this lock?"

"Only one way to find out." Gabe slipped the key into the lock and with one turn it opened. "Well, I guess you've been here before. Anything look familiar?"

She stepped inside, her gaze darting around the dark room. "Not so far. Can we turn on the lights?"

"We'd best not." Instead, Gabe switched on the small flashlight attached to Jinx's key ring. It didn't help much, but he didn't want someone seeing the light and getting suspicious.

The place was small, the living room and kitchen bleeding together into one rectangular room. There was a hallway that Gabe soon learned led to two bedrooms. He quickly checked them out and found them unoccupied.

He breathed a little easier when he saw there was no sign of struggle. No sign to indicate that anything was wrong. Hopefully, that meant Philip was safe.

"Anything?" she asked when he came back into the living room.

Gabe shook his head. In this case, no news might be good news.

He picked up a piece of paper from the small table near the door. "'Jenny, I might be late,'" Gabe read aloud. "'I've got errands to do after I get off from work. Might not see you until breakfast. There are leftovers if you're hungry. Philip.'"

"So, we're alone?" Leigh asked.

"Seems that way."

He heard her pull in her breath. She put her gun aside on the table, shoved her hands in the pockets of her shorts and walked around the living room. He followed her gaze to every piece of furniture, to every knickknack. If she recognized anything, it didn't show in her eyes.

"There are no pictures," she mumbled.

No. Gabe had looked for that when he searched the place. Maybe Philip hadn't wanted to add personal touches because they'd been in hiding.

"I didn't see any women's clothes in the closets either," Gabe explained. He slipped his gun back into the slide holster on his jeans. "So, I guess it's safe to say you didn't live here."

She ran her fingertips over the back of the sofa while she continued to walk around the room. "Maybe Philip can tell me where I do live. If he knows, that is. Maybe I kept it from him, too."

Gabe doubted that. The fact she had a key to the house meant she'd been in contact with her brother.

She groaned softly. "It seems so strange standing here, knowing I should recognize something. Anything. But I don't. With the exception of the few things I've recalled, the only past I know is the one I've made with you these last two days."

And with that, Leigh's gaze skimmed over him.

Something in the air changed. Not the smell of fear and danger that he'd practically grown accustomed to. No. This was a different sensation. A tangle of heat that could only happen between a man and a woman who'd been intimate in just about every way possible.

Gabe didn't even try to talk himself out of the step he took toward her. He reached out. And touched her cheek. Her eyelids fluttered down, and she moved into his touch, letting her lips brush against his fingers.

He could have just gone with the heat. He could have just taken the moment and pushed it until they ended up in bed. Or on the floor. But he wanted to give her more than some flash that was over before they knew what had hit them.

"We have other memories," he said to her. Gabe inched closer, careful to keep a fraction of space between their bodies. That was for his sake, not hers. If she touched him, what control he had left would go straight out the window. "Memories of the first time we kissed."

"Tell me," she whispered.

"It was in the French Quarter. I'd taken you out to do the tourist thing. A date," he added. "I kissed you in the doorway of one of those voodoo parlors. Well, maybe it was more than just one kiss. After about ten or fifteen minutes, the owner said we should get a room."

She smiled, as he'd hoped she would.

"And the first time we made love—that's a memory, too," he continued. In fact, as memories went, that one was as good as it got. "It was on the back porch at my aunt Martha's house near Corpus Christi. A place not much different from this one." His gaze slid around the room before resettling on her. "And we were alone, the only two people for miles around."

"Like now."

"Like now," he confirmed. "Aunt Martha had put

an old bed on that screened porch. I used to like to sleep there when I'd visit her. The place had a tin roof, and it was raining. Not loud, just a summer drizzle, but it made enough noise to blend right in with the sounds of that old bed. The springs were rusty and creaked a little each time we moved.''

''Were the sheets white?'' Leigh asked.

''I think so. Do you remember that?''

''Maybe.'' She shrugged, causing her breasts to brush against his chest. ''Or maybe it's just wishful thinking.''

Now it was his turn to smile. ''My attention wasn't on the color of the sheets. It was on you, Leigh. Completely on you.''

''White sheets,'' she repeated. ''An old bed on a porch. Summer rain. Yes. I think I do remember that.''

With that wistful look on her face, Gabe couldn't resist tasting her. He touched his mouth to hers.

''The place smelled like fresh peaches,'' Gabe's drawl brushed over the words. ''So did we. We'd been picking them right before the rain started. Our clothes were wet by the time we made a run to the porch.''

He might have said more, might have continued the seductive game they were playing if she hadn't caught onto his shoulders. That was all the encouragement he needed to put an end to the talking. He took her mouth instead.

Gabe latched onto a handful of her hair and brought her to him. The kiss was filled with all the fire and heat that had been simmering between them for days.

"This time, I'm not stopping," she mumbled. "I don't care what I remember."

That invitation was just what he wanted to hear. The sound he heard after that, however, wasn't.

Gabe cursed. "Someone's coming," he let Leigh know.

Outside, the dog started to bark.

## *Chapter Fifteen*

Leigh and Gabe unwound themselves from each other immediately and hurried to the window. A bright red compact car stopped directly in front of the house. They barely had time to grab their weapons before she heard someone walking up the steps to the porch.

"Is it Philip?" she whispered.

"Maybe. Don't make a sound."

She hadn't planned to do that, but it soon became apparent that if this was a would-be killer, then he or she was an inept one. The person made enough noise to wake the dead. There was a jangle of keys in the lock and a not-so mumbled string of profanity when the door didn't open right away.

"Get down, Toby," the man yelled. Not an angry yell, exactly. He sounded more annoyed than anything. "Stop it. And don't lick my face, for Christ's sake. You got doggy breath."

"It's Philip," Gabe informed her. That realization, however, didn't cause him to lower his gun.

The door flew open, and the man walked in, still

mumbling under his breath. He reached for the light switch but froze when he realized he wasn't alone. "Holy freaking hell! What are you two trying to do—scare me to death?" Philip pressed a hand over his heart. "How about letting a guy know you're in here before he comes walking in on you?"

Leigh couldn't manage to say anything, but Gabe greeted her brother. "Hello, Philip."

"Gabe." As greetings went, it was rather frosty, but Gabe's had been none too friendly either. "Well, I see you finally found her," Philip commented. "Not that it surprises me. I knew it was just a matter of time."

Philip tossed his keys onto the table and aimed his attention at Leigh. Even though the room was dark, she could still see the concern on his face. "Ever hear of a telephone, sis? It's an amazing invention that allows you to keep in touch with people who are worried sick about you."

Before Leigh could say anything, Philip put his arms around her and pulled her to him. "Now, start explaining," he said in a much softer voice that Gabe probably couldn't hear. "Just what are you doing here with Gabe? And I'm not talking about what you were doing immediately before I walked in. I can figure out that part. What I want to know is what you're *really* doing here with him."

God, where should she start? This wasn't a ten-second explanation. "We have to talk," Leigh simply said. She reached around him and flicked on the light switch.

"Yeah, well, that's what I had in mind, too. A long talk where you do a lot of expla—" His eyes lifted toward the bandage on her head. "What the hell happened to you?"

"It's a long story." She took a deep breath. "Gabe says you're my brother."

Philip stared at her a moment and then made a *yeah, right* sound. She looked at Gabe, silently pleading with him to help with the explanation.

He helped. Gabe spelled it out. "Leigh has amnesia. She doesn't remember much about her life."

Her brother volleyed confused glances between Gabe and her. "Is this some kind of sick joke? Because if it is—"

"It's no joke," she verified.

"Hell." Philip opened his mouth several times as if to add something to that. He finally leaned against the wall and blew out several quick breaths. "Is it temporary?"

She shrugged. "Hopefully. I've started to remember a few things."

"But not me?" Philip tapped his chest. "Not your own brother?"

"No, I'm sorry, I don't."

"But you remember Gabe—"

"No," Leigh interrupted. "I can recall bits and pieces, but I don't remember much about anyone or anything." She took a step closer. "Listen, Philip, how much do you know about what I've been doing for the last two years?"

"A lot. You're my sister, for Christ's sake."

"Then maybe you can answer a few questions. Someone tied me up and tossed me in a lake near New Orleans, and I wondered if you knew anything about it."

His eyes widened significantly, and he cursed. "Someone tried to kill you?"

"Yes. Any idea who might have wanted to do something like that to me?"

"No, of course not." Philip pushed his hand through his sandy-brown hair and made his way to the sofa so he could sit down. "Good God, are you all right?"

"I've been better." At least, she was pretty sure she had been.

Gabe maneuvered her to the chair in front of Philip. "Did Leigh say anything about going to New Orleans?" he asked her brother.

"No. When she came by the club in San Antonio where I work, she told me she had to take a trip, but she didn't say where she was going."

Leigh jumped on that right away. "I was in San Antonio?"

Philip nodded. "Of course. That's where you live. You have a house there."

A house. She finally knew where she lived. Leigh wanted to ask him more, but there were more important things to discuss. "I don't think I'm the only one in danger, Philip. I think you might be in danger, too."

"Yeah, I know. It's to do with those computer searches someone's making."

"You know about that?"

"Sure. That's all you've talked about lately. In fact, you said if you hadn't come back from your trip in three days, I was to call Gabe. I planned to call him this morning."

So, she'd made contingency plans. That meant she had at least considered the possibility that something would go wrong. And it obviously had.

It seemed as if Philip was about to say something else, but the phone rang. He got up from the sofa and checked the caller ID box. "I'll take this call in the bedroom. Nothing critical. Just a friend. I won't be long."

Leigh actually welcomed his departure. She wanted a few moments to regain her composure.

"Are you okay?" Gabe asked. He pulled her into his arms.

"Not really. I have a headache."

"Maybe coffee will help. Come on. I'll make some." He led her into the kitchen and had her sit at the table. Gabe had no sooner reached for the coffee-maker when she heard another car outside. He pulled back the curtain and glanced out the window. "We have company. Get your gun."

Her heart sank. The emotional upheaval of seeing her brother had already drained her, and Leigh now had to force herself to respond to yet another threat.

She snatched her gun from the table and faced the door. Gabe did the same.

"Did you see who it is?" Leigh asked. The dog started to bark again.

"It's a woman, I think. Philip's friend, Jenny. Hopefully."

Yes, Leigh hoped that, too. For a moment anyway. But the hope soon vanished, and what felt like the onset of a panic attack followed. She had no idea what this sudden surge of emotions was all about, but she didn't want Jenny to come through that door.

"Something's wrong," Leigh mumbled.

Gabe glanced at her. "Christ. You're as pale as a ghost. Take a deep breath."

"It won't help," she managed to say. She felt her throat tighten. "Something's wrong."

"Get in the bedroom with your brother. Now! I'll be in there as soon as I'm finished here."

The front door flew open, and because there wasn't time for her to get into the bedroom, Gabe pushed her behind him.

"He stripped off his clothes again on the way over here," the dark-haired woman called out.

She backed through the door and held open the screen with her shoulder. From that angle, she couldn't have possibly seen Leigh or Gabe. Nor did she immediately notice them. Leigh figured that's because the woman had a squirming, nearly naked child in the crook of her arm, and her attention seemed focused on putting a shirt over the child's head.

"I swear, Philip, this kid definitely takes after you," the woman continued. "Are you—"

She turned toward them, her startled blue eyes going from Gabe to the gun he had aimed at her. She reacted quickly, and in a clatter of motion, she tried to swing the child behind her and open her purse.

She wasn't successful at either.

"Who are you?" Gabe asked.

"A friend of Philip's. What have you done to him?" The woman's frightened gaze moved from Gabe to Leigh, and she let out a noisy breath of relief. "Thank God, Leigh, you're here. I didn't even see you back there. You scared me to death."

"Are you Jenny?" Gabe, again. Leigh couldn't seem to make herself speak.

The woman nodded. "And you're Leigh's husband, Gabe. I recognize you from some pictures she has at the house. I didn't know you were coming back with her. I wish I had. I nearly wet my pants when I saw you here with that gun."

"Sorry." Gabe lowered his weapon. "I didn't know I'd be coming. Things just sort of happened that way."

The child began to squirm again, and Jenny placed him on the floor. He broke into a run around the coffee table and stopped right beside Leigh.

"Hi," he said with perfect clarity, and he moved his chubby fingers as if waving at her. With the exception of a diaper, the child was naked.

He tilted his head, causing the loose, dark curls to bounce haphazardly. His wide green eyes held just a hint of mischief. That grin, however, held more than just a hint.

"He's a beautiful child," Leigh said softly, wondering if this was her nephew. But Jenny probably didn't hear her. The woman dropped onto the sofa and closed her eyes, undoubtedly recovering from the fright she'd just had.

Leigh couldn't resist touching those curls, but when she reached out, she remembered that she still held her gun. She quickly lowered it to her side and brushed her fingers through his hair.

The boy pointed toward the bandage on Leigh's head. "Ouchie. Boo-boo. Up, up." He held out his arms for her to take him, and Leigh did, after she put her gun on the bookshelf. She could only guess that he knew her well to go to her so easily.

"What's your name?" she asked, wondering if he was even old enough to tell her.

"Bitty bitty pider," he chattered, repeating the syllables so that they ran together. He gave her a wet, noisy kiss on the cheek.

The kiss made her smile. She didn't know why, but it seemed to be the exact thing she needed. It felt...right.

So incredibly right.

Leigh pulled in her breath and stared at the boy's face. Something was familiar. Something—

"He wants you to sing 'Itsy Bitsy Spider,'" Jenny clarified. The woman placed her purse and the child's clothes on the coffee table. "It's his latest obsession.

He's already had me sing it to him at least three dozen times this morning."

Leigh wasn't sure she remembered the words to that particular song, but it didn't matter. Philip came barreling into the room.

Her brother gave each of them a wild-eyed glance before his attention settled on Jenny. "Did you tell them?"

"Tell them what?" Jenny asked.

"Tell *them,*" Philip emphasized. He gave a series of awkward nods.

Jenny threw her hands up in the air. "I haven't got a clue what you're talking about. I just got here and found Leigh and her husband. Why didn't you tell me she was bringing him back with her?"

"They don't know, all right?" Philip practically shouted. "Leigh has amnesia." And with that, he turned to her. "I didn't want to tell you this way—"

"Tell me what?" Leigh hated that look of fear she saw in his eyes.

"Bitty bitty pider," the child repeated. He caught onto Leigh's cheeks with both hands and tried to force her to give him her attention. She would have if she hadn't instinctively known that Philip was about to tell her something she needed to hear.

"You honestly don't have any memory of this?" Philip asked.

"Of what? Just tell me what's wrong."

Philip gulped in a huge chunk of air. "He's your son."

It took several moments for those words to have any meaning whatsoever. It took even more time for Leigh to sort out that Philip had referred to the little boy in her arms. "My son. This is my son?"

"Your son?" Gabe put his hands on his hips and gave her a scalding look. "What the devil's going on here? You had a baby?" But he didn't wait for her to answer. His gaze swept in Philip's direction.

"*Your* son," Philip clarified. "Yours and Leigh's."

## *Chapter Sixteen*

Oh, God.

Leigh didn't have the energy to become hysterical. Nor the inclination. That probably had something to do with the child she held. Leigh felt only an odd sort of rightness. Something deeper and stronger than a memory. Love, definitely.

Immediate, unconditional love.

One glance at Gabe, however, and she knew he didn't feel that sense of rightness. He looked well past furious, and he was no doubt about to aim all that fury at her.

"Start explaining," Gabe said through clenched teeth.

She cleared her throat. "I take it you don't know about this?"

"No, and so help me, Leigh, you'd better have some answers. Is this my son?"

But Leigh guessed he already had the answer, and it was a definite yes. The boy was a miniature version of Gabe. His hair, his coloring, the shape of his face

Her eyes, though, those green eyes were a genetic copy of her own. She didn't know why she hadn't noticed that when he first came through the door. Or maybe she had. Maybe that's what all those odd feelings were about.

"He's your son." Philip stepped between them. "His name is Houston Gabriel Sanchez."

"Houston," Leigh repeated. She immediately thought of the message she'd left on Gabe's answering machine. *If something goes wrong, get to Philip in Houston.* Except she probably hadn't said *in* but rather *and.* She must have wanted Gabe to protect her brother and her son.

*Their* son.

A son she obviously hadn't told him about.

Oh, God.

"All right, we have some volatile issues to discuss," Philip started. "I want everyone to take a deep breath and calm down."

Following his uncle's instructions, Houston took a loud, exaggerated breath and giggled. He gave Leigh another of those sloppy kisses, and despite the turmoil going on inside her, she returned it.

"I don't want to calm down," Gabe informed Philip. "I want answers. Now, I know Leigh can't remember why she'd mess me over this way, but you know why, Philip. Tell me why you two did this to me."

"I knew it!" Philip aimed a finger at his sister. "Leigh, I don't know how many times I told you this would blow up in your face. And was I right? Obviously.'' He fired his gaze back to Gabe. ''You know how stubborn she can be. I begged her to tell you, and she wouldn't.''

''Why wouldn't I?'' Leigh asked, praying there was a reason she'd understand.

''Because you didn't think it was safe to come out of hiding. You made me swear not to tell him, or you said you'd disappear. Well, I swore to keep your secret and look where it got me, huh? Gabe is about ready to rip out my internal organs. And you know what, Leigh? I don't blame him one little bit for wanting to do that.''

That prompted another round of the song from Houston.

Leigh suddenly felt sick to her stomach. Her son's cheerful song certainly wasn't congruent with what she'd just learned.

Gabe looked ready to yell, but the child must have stopped him. Gabe's mouth twitched. His eyes narrowed to slits. But still he didn't yell. ''Leigh told me the pregnancy was a false alarm,'' he said to Philip.

''That's because the test at the hospital was negative. So, Leigh left thinking there was no baby. But she kept having these symptoms and finally went to another doctor. He confirmed that she was indeed pregnant.'' Philip huffed. ''But before you jump down my throat, Gabe, I didn't know about any of this until almost a year later. Not until Leigh showed up here with Houston.''

Gabe took one calculated step toward Philip. "And at that point you didn't think to call me to let me know that I had a son?"

"Of course I wanted to call you, but Leigh said she would just disappear again. And she could have, too. She was scared, Gabe. She said someone was trying to kill her."

And that was still apparently true. However, Leigh didn't care much for the way she'd handled this situation. Obviously, Gabe didn't either.

She looked at her son's face. "I don't remember anything about him. I don't even know how old he is."

"Eighteen months," Jenny provided. "He was born on Valentine's Day."

That got Gabe looking in the other woman's direction. "I take it you work for Leigh?"

She nodded. "I guess you could say I'm a bodyguard-nanny. I was a cop for six years, and Leigh wanted someone who could protect her son if it came down to that."

So, according to Philip and Jenny, she'd been concerned about safety. Leigh had already known that, since she'd disguised herself, but it was a chilling reminder to realize she'd feared for Houston as well.

Gabe glanced around the room, his gaze landing on her. For a moment. That razor-sharp glare dismissed her and moved back to Jenny. "Do you, Leigh and, uh, Houston all live here?"

"No, we stay at the house in San Antonio."

''But your voice is on Philip's answering machine,'' he reminded her.

''Leigh had me do that because of those computer inquiries about Philip and her. Just a precaution, she said.''

Leigh glanced down at her son, but Houston had his attention solely on Gabe. She saw Gabe glance at the child several times.

''Who?'' Houston asked, pointing toward Gabe.

No one said anything, but their attention all turned toward Leigh. ''It's Daddy,'' she answered, the word sticking in her throat.

It apparently stuck in Gabe's throat as well because he didn't utter a word. Houston did. ''Da-dee. Da-dee,'' he repeated and clapped his hands.

Gabe motioned for her to get up. ''We have to talk. *Now.* Let's go outside.''

''Here, I'll take him,'' Jenny offered, already holding out her hands for the child. Houston went right to her.

''You want me to go with you, sis?'' Philip asked, obviously concerned about Gabe's mood.

Leigh shook her head. ''Thanks though.'' She deserved anything Gabe dished out, and she didn't want an audience for it.

By tacit agreement, they went outside through the back door. Leigh didn't stop walking when she went down the steps and into the yard. She felt as if she would explode if she didn't keep moving, and if she had to look Gabe in the eye. She couldn't imagine what he was feeling right now, but it couldn't be good.

"You should have told me," Gabe let her know as they started down a narrow path away from the house. Thankfully, the dog stayed on the back porch and didn't try to follow them. Leigh didn't want to add the Doberman to what she already had to face.

Gabe kicked at a cluster of dandelion fluff, causing little white umbrellas to scatter everywhere. "You had no right."

"I know. I'm sorry."

He didn't seem to hear her. "How the hell could you do this to me?"

"I don't know." And Leigh really didn't know. If the same scenario played out now, she knew she would tell Gabe about their son. Even if he rejected her and Houston, she would have still told him the truth and relied on him to help her keep their child safe.

They reached a small pond and stopped under a cluster of live oak trees. It was a tranquil place with ducks and lily pads floating on the water. Somewhere in the distance, she could hear wind chimes. It was definitely too tranquil for the storm brewing between them.

"I don't care what your plans were," Gabe continued. "From now on, you *won't* cut me out of my son's life."

No, she wouldn't. Of course, he hadn't mentioned anything about wanting to stay in her life. It didn't surprise Leigh. This was, well, unforgivable. Unforgivable for Gabe. And for her.

"I'M WAITING for an answer," Gabe insisted when Leigh didn't say anything.

Leigh slumped against the tree. "I have no intention of cutting you out of Houston's life again." She slid downward and sat on the ground. "Sweet heaven, you don't think I can justify what I've done, do you?"

"No." He had his fists clenched at his sides, and the veins in his neck felt ready to burst.

She shook her head. "I lied to you. I kept your son from you. What kind of person does something like that, Gabe? No wonder I have amnesia. I don't want to have to remember all the truly rotten things I've done."

That wasn't especially what he wanted to hear. He was spoiling for an argument and didn't want her to concede so easily.

Leigh looked up at him. "Well, say something. Anything. Go ahead and yell at me."

His fists clenched even tighter until he felt his nails dig into his skin. But he couldn't yell. This was a hurt, a wound, that cut all the way to his soul. Yelling wouldn't do a thing to fix that.

"I can see the pain in your eyes." Leigh's voice was the only sound around them. "I don't know how I can ever make it up to you."

"You can't," he snapped.

"I know." She caught her bottom lip between her teeth.

Gabe tried to hang on to the anger, but he felt it slip a considerable notch when he saw a tear spill down her cheek. He slowly lowered himself to the ground beside her. "I hate it when you cry."

She quickly wiped away the evidence. "Sorry." Leigh turned away from him. It didn't fool Gabe. He knew there were still fresh tears in her eyes. "What are we going to do?"

He wished like hell he knew. This wasn't a broken promise or a heated argument. This was his son. He'd lost a year and a half of his son's life, and all because Leigh hadn't trusted him with the truth. She hadn't trusted him to protect them both.

"I don't know a thing about kids," Gabe mumbled. That seemed the least of his worries, but it was a worry. Besides, it seemed less explosive than discussing the other aspects of this issue.

"Neither do I. I don't even know that song he likes. The song Houston likes," she corrected, emphasizing his name. "I don't even know why I named him Houston."

Gabe blew out a long breath. "Probably because that's where you conceived him. If I've done the math right, a little over two years ago we spent a couple of weeks in Houston working on a case. When we were done, we stayed an extra couple of days for a second honeymoon."

She wiped away another tear and glanced at him. "You don't doubt he's your child, do you?"

He felt the muscles in his jaw jump. "No. He's mine." He had no doubts about that. The only doubts he had were about Leigh. "He looks just like me."

"Yes. Except he has my eyes."

Gabe had noticed. He'd never be able to look into Houston's face without seeing Leigh's eyes. DNA sure had a warped sense of humor.

"So, what do we do?" she repeated.

He still wanted to yell and blast her with all the emotions that bounced around inside him. But he was too beat to do that. Besides, Houston added a new wrinkle not only to his personal life but to security measures. Right now, Gabe had to make that his first priority.

"We'll have to deal with all of this later," he let her know. "We can't stay here much longer."

"Yes," she mumbled and then repeated it. "But where will we go?"

"A safe house."

"I shouldn't have to remind you that wasn't the answer for Frank."

"Not an FBI safe house," Gabe corrected. "I have to find out who's trying to kill us. I can't do that if I'm worried about Houston's safety." And hers, of course. He was still too angry to add that part. "My brother has a place near Corpus Christi. He's not there this time of year, so we can use it. Shouldn't take more than a couple of hours to make sure it's safe enough for you and the others to stay there.''

That quickly brought Leigh to her feet. ''Gabe, I don't want to be tucked away in some house while you're out chasing bad guys.''

''That's too bad. The rules have changed. One of us has to watch Houston. Whoever is after you could use him to get to us.''

The color drained from her face. ''You mean the way they tried to use Philip.''

''Worse than that. Philip's a grown man and can take care of himself. My son can't.''

*My son.* The words rang through his head, and Gabe wondered if he would ever be able to say that and not remember the pain Leigh had caused him. At the moment, it sure seemed like too much to hope for.

Leigh pressed her fists against each side of her head. ''This would be so much easier if I just had my memory back. Then I might know who's behind everything.''

That was true, but since they couldn't wait around for that to happen, Gabe had to go about this from a different angle. ''Maybe I can figure it out some other way. There might be something at your house, some kind of information maybe that you've stored in your computer.''

She seemed to give that some thought and then nodded. ''Maybe. After all, I knew someone was making computer inquiries. I had to learn that somehow. Maybe I kept notes.''

It was certainly worth a try. Eventually, they had to get lucky. "I need to work out some arrangements. And I need to call Jinx to let him know what's going on. Houston can stay with Jenny and Philip while you and I make a quick trip to your house. We'll take Philip's car." That way, it might throw off Teresa or anyone else who happened to have a description of Jinx's vehicle. "While we're in San Antonio, I'll have my father arrange for security at my brother's place."

"Yes," she said softly. "And Gabe? For what it's worth, I'm really sorry for not telling you about Houston."

It was worth a hell of a lot. One day, when the anger had faded some, he just might tell her that.

## *Chapter Seventeen*

Leigh hoped a quick shower and a change of clothes would clear her head so she could find something valuable in the information on her computer. So far, neither the shower nor the comfortable cotton dress had worked. She still couldn't find what she needed, but she continued to search through the information while Gabe answered the call that came in on his phone. What she saw on the screen in front of her didn't please her.

There were notes about the computer inquiries—dates and times when the records had been accessed—going back almost the entire two years since she'd disappeared. There was even a summary of the weapons that had been found a few weeks earlier in that raid of the militia compound. She'd apparently known those weapons were from Dayton's original cache. However, what was missing was any speculation about the identity of Dayton's accomplice.

In other words, another dead end.

Of course, she hadn't thought that she'd leave such

sensitive information in a home computer, but Gabe had been right—it was worth a try. It was a good use of time while they waited for his father to set up security at the house in Corpus Christi.

She got up from the computer and stretched. "Nothing," Leigh mumbled under her breath. And that nothing just didn't apply to her computer files either. As she'd done at Philip's, she glanced around the room but didn't recognize anything about the place she'd called home for over a year.

Nothing.

To her brain, it was just a three-bedroom house in a somewhat modest subdivision on the north side of San Antonio. If it hadn't been for the upgraded security system and burglar bars on the windows, it probably would have seemed like the home of any other single mom with a toddler.

To her heart though, the house was much more than that.

It had become her hiding place. A place she'd kept her child from his father. What thought process had she used to reach the point where she would do something like that? Leigh didn't know and wondered if she would ever understand the actions she'd taken.

Behind her, Gabe was on his cell phone with Teresa. Leigh didn't bother to ask how the woman had gotten the number. She'd already learned that Agent Walters was capable of retrieving such things as phone numbers and messages. It was yet one more reason not to trust her.

As if Leigh needed another reason.

If it turned out that Teresa was behind these attempts to kill her, Leigh wouldn't forgive herself for not stopping the woman back in Grand Valley.

She heard Gabe mention two names. Men's names that she didn't recognize, but she knew from other parts of his conversation that they were names of the two people who'd died at the safe house. *Hired guns,* Gabe added. But he didn't seem to have the answer as to who hired them.

She left Gabe in the study and walked through to the adjoining family room. Something squeaked when she stepped onto the thick carpet, and the sound sent her heart racing. It took her a moment to figure out that it was her son's toy turtle. She automatically picked it up and tossed it into the nearby toy box.

Too bad the rest of her problems couldn't be solved so easily.

Gabe had only been back in her life a couple of days. Mere hours. And for all practical purposes, he'd been a stranger when he pulled her out of that lake. At first, she'd distrusted him, argued with him and fought the attraction that had immediately drawn her to him.

And somewhere along the way, she'd fallen in love with him all over again.

Leigh stood there next to her son's toy box and let that sink in. She was in love with Gabe. With her husband. Other than those who claimed love at first sight, this was probably some kind of record. It certainly didn't make things easier, especially since she had no idea if Gabe and she could even have a future together.

So, the real question was—what was she going to do about it? Or better yet, what would Gabe do about it? Would he even consider forgiving her? Would he risk giving her another chance?

She turned and walked back through the kitchen to find him, but Gabe wasn't in the study where she'd left him. Leigh didn't panic. She knew he wouldn't leave her alone in the house. He'd probably come to the same conclusions she had about the information on the computer—that it wasn't helpful—and decided there was no reason to keep staring at the screen.

Leigh followed the hallway to the end and found him in Houston's bedroom. The walls had been painted sunshine yellow, and there was a double bed next to the crib. She'd likely spent many nights sleeping in her son's room, probably because she'd feared for their safety.

Gabe's back was to her, his gaze focused on something on the dresser. She glanced over his shoulder to see what had captured his attention. It was a photograph of Gabe.

"Thank you for that," he said without looking back at her.

"It seems a paltry substitute now. I must have been scared. I'm not trying to make excuses, because I know what I did was wrong. It was stupid not to trust you to protect us." Frustrated with his silence, and her own babbling, Leigh shook her head. "Look, I wish you'd just yell or something and get it over with. I know you're furious but—"

"Yeah, I am," he snapped.

She waited for more. But that seemed to be the sum total of what should have been a tirade. Gabe certainly had a right to a vent and rant.

"That's it? That's all you're going to say?" Leigh demanded. God, she was practically picking a fight, but she couldn't stand the silent treatment any longer. She deserved to be yelled at. "Will you at least look at me?"

He did. Gabe eased around to face her. And face her, he did. Leigh immediately regretted that she'd issued such a demand. There was something almost dangerous in the depths of those fiery blue eyes, and there was definitely something unnerving about the way he combed his gaze over her.

Gabe took a single step toward her, nearly halving the distance between them. The room suddenly seemed very, very small. And where had the air gone?

Leigh held her ground. Barely. "What are you going to do?" She felt her pulse sprint out of control. Not from fear. Not this. This was something that stirred deep within her blood.

His gaze never left hers. "Get on the bed."

She'd braced herself to hear Gabe say or shout almost anything. But not that. Certainly not that. Sweet heaven. The timing was all wrong.

Wasn't it?

Then, why did she feel that slow melting heat slide down the length of her entire body?

He caught onto her arm and maneuvered her to the bed. "Sit down. I want to check your bandage."

"Oh." That. Just that. Leigh tried to force herself not to be disappointed. Or scream. After all, the timing reeked for practically everything that had crossed her mind in the last thirty seconds. And a lot of things had crossed her mind.

Gabe stooped, pulled her foot into his lap and unwound the bandage. "When you get to my brother's house, you'll need a doctor to take a look at this."

"Of course."

"It seems to be healing," he continued. "But it wouldn't hurt to have those stitches checked."

"Sure." Leigh groaned when she heard her polite, clinical tone. It matched Gabe's to a tee, but it was nowhere near a match for what she was feeling inside. "If you yell at me, it might make you feel better."

He rewrapped the bandage and kept his attention focused solely on that. "Why are you so anxious to hear me raise my voice, huh?"

"Because I'm hoping it'll get us talking again. Really talking. And I don't mean this chitchat stuff either. I mean a real, pertinent discussion about us, and about our son."

Gabe looked up at her. And looked. She did her own share of looking and liked everything she saw. The man certainly had her hormonal number. Probably a conditioned response to all those times he'd made love to her. Or maybe she'd always reacted this way to him. It was like being micro-zapped with a lethal dose of testosterone.

"You want to talk, Leigh?" he asked, his words slow and deliberate. He kept his gaze fixed right on her while he tugged off the sandals that she'd put on after her shower. He let the shoes drop to the floor.

Gabe still had her foot in his lap, and with that same slow and deliberate pace, he slid his hand over the inside curve of her ankle. And he just kept moving up. Inch by inch. One unhurried caress at a time. His touch was hot, arousing. And effective.

His hand came to a stop at the back of her knee. "Well?" he prompted. "Is that what you want?"

Leigh tried to answer him, even though she had no idea what to say. Leave it to Gabe to render her speechless. She settled for shaking her head.

"Know what I think?" he went on. That clever hand began to move again. Adding some slight pressure, he slid his fingers from her knee onto her thigh. He pushed up her dress along the way, baring her skin to his touch. "I think we could talk and yell until there's no breath left in us. But what would we accomplish?"

She shook her head again, aware of the instant energy that simmered between them. "Gabe—"

"It wouldn't accomplish much." He brushed his thumb over the little spot just above the back of her knee.

Leigh's breath shuddered. She shoved her palms

against the mattress to keep herself from falling backward and just looked at him. His face, strong and angled. Handsome. Those intense eyes. The shape of his sensual mouth. His bronze-colored hand resting against the inside of her thigh.

He shifted his weight until he was kneeling between her legs, and he leaned in closer. Leigh felt his warm breath brush over her. He was nearly touching her panties. But not quite. It was that *not quite* that made her want to ask for more. Much, much more.

"I mean, what's there to say?" Gabe asked. "You feel the need to keep telling me you're sorry. Heck, I know that already. Just like you know when everything is said and done, we'll figure out a way to work through what's happened."

"We will?" she managed to say, though it had little sound.

He touched his mouth to the inside of her thigh. "We will."

She hissed when that touch turned to a full-fledged kiss. *Oh, my.* Her heart pounded. And she suddenly wanted him more than her next breath.

His hand went higher, bunching up her dress until both his hand and the loose cotton stopped at the juncture of her thighs. He lowered his head again. Paused. And snared her gaze once more. His eyebrow arched in what would normally be a questioning gesture. But there were no questions in his suddenly smoky eyes.

"What are you planning to, um, do?" she asked.

That dark eyebrow went up a notch more. "What do you think I'm planning to do?"

A few answers came to mind, incredibly satisfying answers, but he didn't wait for her to voice them. Nor did Gabe wait for her to brace herself for the erotic onslaught. He kissed the bare skin just below the edge of her white lacy panties. Slowly. Thoroughly. He nipped the tender flesh with his teeth. Leigh gasped and caught onto his shoulders.

And he didn't stop there.

Adding considerable breath, Gabe moved his mouth across the front of her panties. Where he lingered, and kissed, a while. Before making his way to her stomach. He circled her navel with his tongue.

"Did I make my intentions clear?" he asked.

She nodded, the movement of her head jerky and frantic. "Definitely."

"I thought so."

He reached out and slid his hand around the back of her neck—capturing her and her breath. Everything went still and hazy. Except for his face. His mouth came to hers.

Gabe took everything she offered him. Everything. The kiss wasn't gentle, nor did she want it to be. It carried with it the years of want. Need. And desire. Leigh let herself be swept away.

He didn't stop or even slow down. Gabe, too, seemed to know exactly what would happen here, and he wouldn't ask for permission. He took those scorching kisses to her cheek. Her throat. His mouth moved over her as if he knew every secret she'd ever had. Maybe he did. Maybe that was part of the magic created between them.

Despite the horror of the day, and the uncertainty of their future, this was right.

Leigh pulled off his T-shirt and slid her hand down his bare chest. She felt the tight muscles, his warm skin, the rapid thump of his heart. It beat to the same rhythm as hers. And the memories of them together came flooding back.

The eager touches.

The long kisses.

Need that just wouldn't go away.

"Still want to talk?" he asked.

Leigh curved her arm around him. "No way."

GOOD. Gabe wasn't exactly in the mood for conversation either. Maybe later. Much, much later.

He snapped Leigh to him so he could feast on her mouth. He took. And took. But soon that wasn't enough.

"More," he demanded.

The slow, eating hunger that had always been there had a new urgency. This time he'd do something about it.

She fought with his jeans as he fought with her clothes. By default he won since her loose dress wasn't much of a barrier. He pulled it over her head and sent it flying across the room. Gabe took one look at her and nearly lost his breath.

Leigh sat there in front of him. Naked, except for the flimsy lace bra and panties. He could see right through those. And she was perfect. Absolutely perfect. The subtle scent of her arousal, and his, stirred around them.

"Do you remember how it was between us?" he asked.

The corner of her mouth lifted. "Remind me."

Oh, he planned to do that all right. That and more. Gabe slid his hand from the base of her throat to her bra. He opened the clasp and pushed the swatch of lace from her breasts. He didn't waste any time before he touched her.

A low sound rumbled in her chest. She grabbed onto his shoulders and pulled him even closer. "You're very good at this," Leigh let him know.

Gabe slid his fingers over her breasts. She felt like warm, wet silk. "*We* were always good at this."

"Really?" Her breath hitched when he captured her nipple between his thumb and forefinger. He gave it a gentle pinch. "Because I'm thinking this isn't a *we* kind of accomplishment here. You're the one who's doing the touching and kissing in all the right places. And trust me, you are very, very good at it."

He took her hand and placed it on his chest. "You're welcome to do all the touching and kissing you want."

She did. Somehow, Gabe knew she would. She watched his face while she ran her hand down his stomach. It was distracting, along with feeling damn good.

While he still had a little self-control left, he lowered his head and sampled her breasts. When his mouth closed over her nipple, she arched against him. Seeking more. And finding it.

It didn't, however, stop the downward progress of her hand.

She eased her nimble fingers right over the front of his jeans. Hell. That little maneuver caused him to see double, but he had no trouble seeing her wicked little smile.

"You're right," she assured him. "*We* are very good at this. Let's see just how good we can get."

The woman caught on too damn fast. He cursed and crushed his mouth to hers while she fumbled with his jeans. She finally succeeded in getting them unzipped. Leigh pushed them off his hips and slid her hand inside his boxer shorts.

Gabe managed a hoarse groan when she wrapped her fingers around him. What was left of his self-control shattered into a million pieces. He had to have her—now. He latched onto her hips and stripped off her panties.

He eased her back onto the soft mattress, ridding himself of the jeans and boxers along the way. Naked, he joined her on the bed.

"Now," she insisted.

Gabe very much wanted *now,* but he also needed to touch her. He needed to watch her respond to him in the most basic way. He slid his hands across her lower stomach and drew back her leg slightly so he could caress the inside of her thigh with his fingertips.

Leigh moaned. Her eyelids fluttered and threatened to close, but somehow she kept her focus on him.

"Gabe." It was a plea. And more.

He gave her back everything she'd just given him with that promise he saw in her eyes. "Leigh. You're mine, understand? You'll always be mine."

He wasn't even sure she heard him, and there was no time for him to repeat it. Repositioning her, Gabe moved his hand and eased into that slick soft heat.

Leigh caught onto his shoulders and brought him even closer so they could complete the union. Her body adjusted, too.

She met his powerful thrusts, creating a rhythm between them that was unique but at the same time as old as time. He gave her exactly what she needed to coax her to fulfillment.

Friction. Pressure. Thrust after penetrating thrust.

He moved in and out, across the sensitive bud of flesh and deeply inside so that every inch of her body felt him.

Gabe felt her need rise and surged, coiling until it was no longer insistent but necessary. She said his name and added a mumbled plea, a primitive demand for completion. Driving faster, harder, deeper, he gave her what they both demanded. What they both needed.

When he could go no higher and take no more, Gabe did the only thing he could do. He surrendered. And took her with him.

# *Chapter Eighteen*

Leigh lay in his arms. Happy. Content. Peaceful. She was afraid to speak for fear of breaking the spell. She wanted to hold on to as much of the moment as she could.

One perfect moment. Well, several of them, actually. That thought made her smile. Yes, there were definite advantages to being naked in Gabe's arm. And having him naked in hers.

"Please tell me you're not having second thoughts," Gabe mumbled.

"No second thoughts."

"Good." He reached over, slid his fingers into her hair and pulled her mouth to his for another taste.

Leigh made a shameless sound of satisfaction and ran her tongue over her bottom lip to savor the kiss. "Since you kissed me in the clinic, I've always wondered about having sex with you—again. How it would be." She paused long enough to push his hair off his forehead. "And now I know."

"Not so fast." He gave his head a shake and eased

right into his Texas drawl. "We didn't have sex, *mi vida.* We made love."

"And the difference is?"

"The people involved."

Leigh blinked. It wasn't an answer she'd expected, but it was certainly one she'd wanted. There was absolutely nothing about this that was ordinary.

He pulled her to him and kissed her again, a reminder of what was at stake here. Not that she needed such reminders. The reminder was there. It was something almost tangible between them. Emotion barely masked with a slick coating of fire. Nor was it likely to go away anytime soon. Everything they'd been through, all the disappointments and danger, hadn't been able to diminish it.

"You're thinking too much," he mumbled as if reading her thoughts.

Yes, she was. She didn't want to think about the challenges still facing them. Leigh didn't want reality intruding on this moment. Their moment. Gabe's and hers. Still, in the back of her mind, there was the doubt. The one question that she just couldn't seem to shut out.

What now?

Leigh settled deeper into Gabe's arms, knowing they had only a few more minutes before they had to get up. Since they hadn't been able to find anything on her computer, they'd need to get back to Philip's and get ready for the trip to Corpus Christi. She prayed Gabe's father would be as thorough with those security arrangements. She didn't want to take any more chances with her son's life.

She closed her eyes, and the image of Houston came to mind. Houston taking a nap on the quilt in the family room. She smiled at the serene memory.

But her smile soon faded.

Another picture slowly overshadowed that peaceful one. An image of murky darkness. Raw smells. And sounds that chilled her to the bone.

Leigh gasped.

"What's wrong?" Gabe asked.

She felt him move, probably so he could see her face, but Leigh wasn't able to answer him. The memories came flooding back in a jumbled heap. And the heap wasn't pleasant.

"The gun jammed," she heard herself say. But she didn't actually see a gun. It was the sound. That click. Followed by muffled profanity.

"What gun, Leigh?"

She forced her eyes to open to stop the speeding images, and she saw Gabe. As comforting as that was, it didn't soothe the storm inside her. "At the lake where I was supposed to meet you. I remember the gun jammed."

He studied her eyes for a moment. "Who tried to kill you? Do you know who Dayton's accomplice is?"

She shook her head to both questions. "I don't know." As painful as it was, Leigh closed her eyes again and let the images come. And they came all right. It was a deluge of everything that she thought she'd forgotten. ''When I got to the lake, I could see a car down the shore. I thought it was yours. I parked behind it, but when I stepped out, I heard a shot and felt something graze my head.''

Gabe cursed. It was no doubt as hard for him to hear this as it was for Leigh to relive it. ''And then what happened?'' he asked.

''I fell, and that's when I heard the click. The gun jammed.''

He got to a sitting position and put his head against the backboard. ''So, you're alive because the gun jammed.''

That made her lucky. But it hadn't felt much like luck at the time.

''I must have passed out,'' she continued, trying to pick through everything and explain what had happened. ''When I came to, I was already in the water. And you know the rest.''

''Some of it,'' he corrected. He mumbled something under his breath. ''I guess you called me because I thought I could help you find out who was making those computer inquiries. Or maybe because of those weapons that had surfaced. Too bad I didn't get to that bridge a couple of minutes sooner. I might—''

''I didn't call you just because I needed your help.''

The next image that came into her head wasn't one of darkness and jammed guns. It was her making that phone call to Gabe.

''I called you from a pay phone so I could tell you about Houston.'' Leigh went on. ''I'd planned to tell you everything. But then I thought someone was watching me. I got scared and rattled off that part about you meeting me. And that part about Houston. I knew you wouldn't know what it meant, but I didn't have time to explain."

He didn't say anything, but when Leigh looked at him she understood why. The news had touched him as much as it'd touched her. She'd planned to tell Gabe about his son. It was almost two years late, but there was some comfort in knowing she'd tried to do the right thing.

"Thank you," he whispered.

She nodded, not trusting her voice.

Gabe rubbed his hands over his face. "What else do you remember?"

Leigh sifted through the images, sounds and thoughts that were still going through her head. "Everything, I think."

"Everything?"

"Yes."

Leigh was almost afraid that the mere admission would make the memories go away again. But it didn't. She tested herself. She remembered her childhood. The first time Gabe had kissed her in the French Quarter. She even remembered the bed on the back porch at Aunt Martha's.

The sheets had been white. They had smelled of fresh peaches and rain.

She remembered Gabe's parents, the easy way they had welcomed her into the Sanchez family. She remembered giving birth to Houston. Holding him. Nursing him. And she even remembered the incredible guilt she'd felt because she believed the only way to keep her son safe was to stay in hiding.

"It's all there," she let him know. The happiness. The sadness. Her life.

Gabe hesitated a moment before he pulled her back into his arms. "Good."

He might have said more, might have even discussed where they would go from there, but the phone rang, taking away the rest of the moment.

"That'll be my father." He reached for the phone. "The house is probably ready."

Ready, as in they'd have to leave. She got off the bed and started to dress. It was just as well. Leigh was anxious to get back to Houston. Besides, she hoped there would be other times—in the very near future—when Gabe and she would make love again.

"Hell," Gabe said only moments after answering the phone.

Leigh stopped, her arm just partway through the sleeve of her dress. "What's wrong?"

Gabe didn't answer her, but she knew from his expression that something horrible had happened. He motioned for her to move closer to the phone.

"Please, God," she prayed. "Don't let anything be wrong with Houston."

With that prayer still fresh on her lips, Leigh leaned closer to the phone and heard something that turned her world upside down.

"I WANT TO END THIS quickly," the mechanical voice continued. It was so distorted, Gabe couldn't tell if it was a man or a woman. It didn't matter. The greeting had been more than enough for Gabe to know this person meant business.

*I have your son. And the others. They'll die if you don't do as I tell you.*

Leigh had no doubt heard that part. Her gasp let Gabe know she didn't handle the news any better than he had.

"Who is this?" Gabe didn't figure he'd get an answer to that question, and he was right.

"Leigh should have been dead now. Put her on the phone. I need to speak to her."

"You'll speak to *me,*" Gabe insisted. "What the hell do you want?"

"Put Leigh on the phone. I hate to be dramatic, but if you don't, your son will die right now."

He hadn't thought anything could scare him more, but that did it. Cursing the fact that he didn't have a choice, Gabe slowly passed the phone to Leigh. "This...person has Houston."

He watched the terror pass through her eyes. "How can that be?" She grabbed the phone. "What have you done with my son?" she yelled.

Gabe pressed his face close to hers so he could hear the person's response. It was a response that didn't give him much comfort. "The boy's safe. For now. Please help me keep it that way."

"Start talking," Leigh demanded.

"I have all four of them. Your son, Jenkins, your brother and the woman. They can't identify me. None have seen my face. All of them will be perfectly safe if you do as I say."

Leigh caught onto Gabe's hand and met his gaze. "What do you want me to do?" she asked the caller.

"I'll exchange you for your son. I promise to make it quick and painless, not like at the lake. Meet me at your brother's house. Park the car at the end of the road by the mailbox, put your hands on your head and walk toward the house. I'm giving you exactly one hour, Leigh. If you're even one minute late, I'll kill them all. And this time, I can promise you that the gun won't jam."

Because Gabe was so close to her, he saw the pulse jump in her throat. She almost managed to suppress the groan. Almost. But the groan was warranted. It was about a thirty- to forty-minute drive back to Philip's, and that was only if they drove as fast as they could. That gave them precious little time.

Still, when she spoke, Leigh kept the fear that Gabe knew she felt out of her voice. "Using my son wasn't smart. In fact, I'd say that was about the biggest mistake you could make."

"No, *you* made the mistake. By the way, if you're thinking about bringing Agent Sanchez with you, think again. If I see him within ten miles of this place, every one of you will die. Now, let me speak to him."

Leigh handed him the phone, but she didn't listen to the conversation. She hurriedly began to change her clothes, grabbing a pair of jeans and a shirt from the closet. With the phone cradled against his ear, Gabe dressed as well while the kidnapper rattled off yet more instructions. Instructions that would supposedly save his son.

And get his wife killed.

Gabe listened carefully, dissecting each word and each step of his orders. Before he could try to buy them some more time, however, the caller hung up.

He didn't waste any time with more profanity. "I'm supposed to leave now to find Philip," he relayed to Leigh. "He's tied up somewhere out in the middle of nowhere with an explosive device strapped to him. If I'm not there in an hour, he dies."

"Oh, God." Even though the horror of their situation was on her face, she didn't give in to it. "So, what do we do?"

Gabe thought about it for a moment, praying the fog would clear out of his head. Damn this person. He'd faced plenty of danger before but never when his wife's and son's lives were at stake. "This is all a ploy to separate us. Whoever's doing this won't let you just walk out of there."

"I know. For whatever reason, this person wants me dead."

He finished putting on his clothes, grabbed his gun and started for the car. Leigh was right behind him. He got them on the road, speeding toward Philip's, before he reached for his phone. "I'll call someone to go after your brother."

"But if the kidnapper sees you—"

"That won't happen." It couldn't happen. Gabe would just have to find a way around that.

He called the field office and explained everything so they would send someone to find Philip. It was a huge gamble. Philip might die simply because he wouldn't be the one to rescue him, but Gabe couldn't justify leaving Leigh and his son at the mercy of a killer.

"There's someone who wants to talk to you," the other agent informed Gabe.

"Who?" His first thought was the kidnapper had called the field office, but it wasn't the artificial voice he heard on the phone. It was Teresa.

"I listened in on your call to request backup," she let Gabe know. "I was already on my way out to Philip O'Brien's house so I could meet with Jinx. I'll see what I can do to stop this."

Hell. Couldn't he even manage to get a secure line to a field office? However, Gabe had too many other things to worry about without being riled about that. "What'd you do—plant another transmitter so you could keep tabs on us?"

"No, but someone planted one in Jinx's car. I've been tracking you since Grand Valley. That's how I knew where Philip lived. I called Jinx when I realized where you were going, and he drove straight out to check on Philip and the others. When he didn't call back, I got concerned."

Gabe didn't even care if she was telling the truth.

"This is none of your business, Teresa. Just stay out of it."

"Whoever took those hostages might be connected to Dayton's accomplice. That makes it my business."

Maybe. But he had priority. Because this was personal.

He hung up, ignoring her rather loudly spoken orders that he would cooperate. If he was wrong about Teresa, if she was truly the person behind the kidnapping, then he'd deal with her soon enough. But if she was just trying to do her job, then maybe she wouldn't get in the way of him stopping the kidnapper.

"Teresa knows what's going on?" Leigh asked.

Gabe nodded. "She says she's on her way to Philip's." He gave her the summary of what Teresa had told him.

"I don't like it." Leigh checked the magazine in her gun. "She could be lying about a transmitter being in Jinx's car. You think this is all just a ruse to make us think she's not the kidnapper?"

"Could be." He took out more ammunition from the compartment beneath the seat and passed it to her. "But it doesn't matter who we're up against. We still have to get onto Philip's property without being seen."

"Any idea how?"

"Once we're near the house, we'll leave the car," Gabe told her. "Then we'll cut through the woods and get to the house from the back."

"But the kidnapper will probably expect us to do that."

"Then we'll be careful." It was an inadequate postscript, but it was all Gabe could offer her. "We'll have to split up when we cut through the woods." He pulled off his watch and passed it to her.

"What's this for?"

"I can use the clock on the phone to keep track of time. That way, if one of us gets caught, the other will still have a chance to get to the house."

Leigh only nodded, apparently understanding what had to happen. One of them had to get to Houston in time. And it didn't matter what the cost. Damn. It was like sending his wife in front of a firing squad. It brought home too many painful memories. He felt as helpless as he had the day someone had kidnapped his sister.

"I'll take the side by the pond. You take the other," Gabe continued, trying to push the thoughts of his sister away. He tried to think of all contingencies. "If there's a trail, don't follow it. Stay in the brush and keep low. If you can, get to the house from the back or side, and if you make it that far, go in through the window."

"Okay." She took a deep breath. "You think this person is someone we know?"

"Could be."

"Maybe Frank or Teresa. Or maybe even Jinx?"

He didn't think it was Jinx, but Gabe couldn't rule out the other two. After all, someone had spent the past two days trying to kill them. ‘‘I won’t ask you to change your mind about him, but Jinx is on our side, Leigh. I’d stake my life on that.’’

‘‘Well, that’s exactly what you’re doing, isn’t it? You’re staking your life. Mine. And your son’s.’’

Yes. He was. Gabe turned off the main highway and headed up the country road that would take him to Philip’s house. Maybe it was the thoughts of his sister or perhaps the memory of Dayton’s attempt to kill Leigh, but Gabe felt that tingle in the back of his head. It was a warning that something beyond the obvious wasn’t right.

Hell.

He hoped he was right about Jinx. But hope suddenly didn’t seem enough. Not nearly enough. He couldn’t risk Leigh’s and Houston’s lives on hope.

‘‘Don’t trust anyone but me,’’ he amended. ‘‘All right?’’

She made a sound of contemplation. And then agreement. Leigh lay her gun on the seat and strapped on his watch. ‘‘What if we don’t make it to the house on time?’’

‘‘If time is running out, I’ll go in no matter what.’’ Gabe stopped the car near a spot of heavy brush and stepped out.

Leigh got out also and looked at him over the hood. She swallowed hard. ‘‘In case I don’t make it back—’’

‘‘Don’t.’’

But she ignored him. ‘‘No, this is too important. If

I don't make it back, let Houston know I love him. Okay?''

''Okay.'' The word nearly didn't make it out of his throat. There wasn't time for reassurance or even for a proper goodbye. Each second counted. Gabe had already started to sprint up the road when he heard Leigh call out to him.

''And Gabe? Just for the record—I love you, too.''

She didn't give him time to respond. Not that there was time. She lifted a hand in farewell and disappeared into the thick woods.

# Chapter Nineteen

Leigh shoved away the low limbs of a hackberry tree and ducked underneath to run deeper into the woods. She'd left Gabe just minutes earlier. Six minutes, to be precise.

It felt more like a lifetime.

Streaky sunlight pierced through the thick overhead branches, so she could see where she was running. Barely. She'd already stumbled a few times. Thankfully, she had on a pair of sneakers she'd gotten from her house. If not, the flip-flops would have certainly slowed her down.

All around her were the smells of rotting leaves, mold and earthworms. It was Texas-hot, and sweat snaked its way down her face and back. Thankfully, she wasn't in physical pain. Her ankle was past the hurting stage. Now, it was just numb.

Things certainly weren't looking good. She had no real plan for Houston's rescue. Her son's abductor, however, probably had a well-thought-out scheme, one that no doubt included her death. And maybe Gabe's, too. But her own life meant nothing if she couldn't save them.

There were nineteen minutes left of the time the kidnapper had allotted her. At the pace she was running, she would probably make it to the house with twelve minutes to spare. Twelve very valuable minutes. It would give her time to consider her options and decide what to do. And she did have options, few that they were.

Of course, all scenarios were dangerous and could potentially end the same way—a deadly shoot-out with her child caught in the middle. Still, they existed, and that's what she had to concentrate on. Walking straight into the gunman's waiting arms was one way. She might get off a shot before he or she did.

*Might.*

And if not, then Gabe was her backup plan. She would gladly sacrifice herself if it'd give Gabe time to get to Houston.

She crossed a grassy hill and stopped at a gully not too far from the house. Because it hadn't rained recently, it was little more than a wide dusty ditch that made a beeline toward the barn. Using the thick cedars for cover, she peeked at the house, hoping to get a glimpse of her son.

Nothing.

The place looked deserted, and much too quiet.

The woods weren't quiet though. Overhead, some blue jays squawked. The wind agitated the leaves and branches. Her heart seemed to make the most noise of all—it pounded in her ears and throat.

Leigh moved closer, staying behind the trees for cover. The low, rumbling growl, however, stopped her in her tracks.

"Not now," she whispered. "Please don't let it be Philip's dog."

She fought against the instinct to run, and at the same time, she tried not to make any sudden moves. Leigh turned slowly in the direction of the sound. It was just as she feared. The dog inched his way toward her.

The animal's oil-black eyes immediately connected with hers. He growled again. She had no time to waste on this, and she couldn't very well fire a warning shot to get him to move away. To save her son, she had to get past that dog. And one way or another, she would.

"Sit!" she whispered.

The dog tilted his head, silently quizzing her. He still had his teeth bared though, so she repeated her command. This time he relaxed his jaw and sat.

Leigh quickly tried to level her breathing. She couldn't risk hyperventilation, nor could she risk being late. She checked the watch—time was running out.

A sliver of motion caught her eye. Whatever it was, it disappeared behind the remains of an old stone fence that meandered through the woods. If it was the kidnapper, then he or she couldn't have moved that fast with a child in tow. Especially not an active child like Houston.

So, where was her son?

In the house, maybe. But the kidnapper wouldn't have gotten too far away from the hostages. The person wouldn't have wanted to take a chance on losing a bargaining chip. That meant her son was probably close by. But where? And if he was close, then why hadn't she heard him?

Leigh quickly pushed that question aside. She already had too much to deal with without adding that.

"Leigh?" someone called out. The voice was hardly more than a whisper.

It was Jinx. *Jinx.* What in the name of God was he doing out here? The kidnapper wouldn't have just let him go.

Unless he was the kidnapper.

Every muscle in her body went stiff. "Where are you?" she risked asking.

"Over here."

He'd moved. His voice came farther from the right that time. Leigh moved, too. Toward him. It was a risk, since he might very well be the person who wanted her dead, but it would be more of risk to her son if she didn't face the kidnapper head-on.

"Houston's out here...somewhere," she heard Jinx say.

She'd figured that out already. Piles of leaves crunched with each step she took, and their sound probably gave away her position. There was nothing she could do about it. She only hoped it would work both ways, and that Jinx wouldn't be able to backtrack and sneak up on her.

"Teresa's here too somewhere," Jinx added.

Leigh had no time to react to that news. The birds suddenly became too quiet. She dropped to her stomach and listened. When she heard the snap of a twig, she rolled over and came up on one knee, prepared to fire.

Nothing.

However, she heard something else. A swishing sound. Someone shooting a gun rigged with a silencer. But who was the shooter, and what were they shooting at?

She didn't like the answer that came to her.

"Please, not Houston or Gabe," she said to herself.

But it wasn't helplessness that she felt. Anger slammed through her, quickly replacing the fear. Raising her gun into the air, Leigh fired and yelled. The sound she made was nothing coherent, just something to divert attention from her husband and her son. She had no idea if it'd work, but she lowered her weapon to eye level again.

And waited.

She wasn't sure how much time passed. Probably mere seconds. She didn't dare let down her guard to check the watch Gabe had given her.

"Stay down, Leigh," Gabe shouted.

She almost panicked at the sound of his voice. God, she prayed he wasn't out in the open.

The bushes behind her rattled. Leigh reeled toward

them just as a rock thudded to the ground only yards away. She spun back to her original position, cursing the fact that she couldn't cover all sides at once.

She saw someone race behind a tree. A man. She kept her attention on the spot where she'd seen him disappear, and soon he stepped out again. At first, Leigh thought she was seeing things, but she recognized the rusty-red hair and pencil-slim build. It was Frank Templeton. He had a piece of rope dangling from his left wrist. Had he been taken captive and managed to escape?

Hurried footsteps suddenly seemed to be all around her, so Leigh forced her gaze from Frank. She decided to hold position where she was.

As if obeying some silent command, the dog suddenly sprang to his feet, bolted in front of Leigh and disappeared into the brush. She didn't know whether to be relieved or not. Maybe the animal would attack the person who'd kidnapped Houston.

There was nothing muffled about the next shot. It blistered through the woods with an ear-piercing blast and came right at her. It clipped a small branch less than an inch from her head.

The next shot sliced across her arm and grazed her skin. Leigh dropped. Rolled to her stomach. And raised her gun to defend herself.

A FLURRY OF ACTIVITY was all around him. Gabe tore through the brush toward Leigh, who was still on the ground. He glanced at her for only a split second before he turned toward the direction of the shots and aimed.

"Are you all right?" he whispered.

"Yes. You?"

He nodded without taking his attention off their surroundings. He was well past being furious. How dare someone, anyone, take a shot at Leigh. Now, if he could just figure out who'd done such a stupid thing, then he would pulverize them. Unfortunately, time wasn't on his side. He had about eight minutes to figure it all out.

That eight minutes came sooner than he planned.

He saw Jinx emerge from a pocket of bushes about twenty yards ahead. Jinx apparently saw him too because he started toward them. His friend was armed, a sleek black pistol gripped in his hand. If this was a man Gabe shouldn't trust, then he needed to do something about it right away.

But what?

"Is Leigh all right?" Jinx called out.

Gabe didn't answer immediately. "No, she's not breathing."

The lie had barely left his mouth when Gabe heard the rustle behind them. Footsteps. Slow. Cautious. He hauled Leigh off the ground and spun her around so they were back to back, the same stance they'd used when they escaped the clinic. This time, however, he didn't order her to shoot to kill. He couldn't. He couldn't risk shooting their son.

It seemed the footsteps converged toward them at

the same pace as Jinx's. Gabe knew they wouldn't have to wait long. Whatever would happen, would happen soon.

In front of Jinx, a flock of doves sputtered into the air and darted in all directions. Barking, the dog bolted forward to chase them. From his right, Gabe heard yet another person approach.

Teresa Walters.

He'd already seen Frank, so that meant all the players were in place. Knowing that, Gabe decided what he had to do.

"Get down, Leigh!" Gabe shouted.

Catching her arm with his elbow, he pushed her back to the ground and turned. The moment he saw the figure and where the person had the weapon aimed, Gabe fired.

"Oh, God." With her gun still ready, Leigh came up on her knee and aimed in the direction where Gabe had shot. Jinx raced to her side and did the same.

Frank stumbled forward just as his gun fired into the ground. With a bright red stain quickly spreading over his shoulder, he fell. He wasn't dead though.

And he had his gun aimed right at Leigh.

Grimacing, Frank went to fire again, but Gabe stopped him. He didn't want the man dead—yet—but he definitely intended to stop him. Gabe sent a bullet into Frank's right wrist. The second shot propelled the gun from his hand.

"I wouldn't if I were you," Gabe warned when

Frank reached for his gun. He aimed right at Frank's head.

Jinx quickly retrieved the gun that Frank had dropped and restrained him.

"Where's Houston?" Leigh asked.

"I saw him. He's fine," Jinx assured her.

She nodded, obviously accepting his answer and turned to Gabe. "How did you know it was Frank?"

"He was the one person who *shouldn't* have been out here."

With all the worry about Leigh and Houston, it'd taken Gabe a while to figure that out. Jinx had already been on the scene, and Gabe had spoken to Teresa himself. That left Frank. There was no logical explanation as to why he would be in the woods behind Philip's house.

Fire flashed through her eyes, and Leigh whirled toward Frank. "Why did you do this?"

He actually smiled at her. "Because you knew where the storage facility was."

"I didn't." She shook her head and repeated it softly. "I had no idea. I only saw one word in the address—Texas."

"But I couldn't take that chance, could I? I knew you would eventually figure it out. I did, even though it took me nearly two years to check out every potential storage facility in the Dallas area."

Dallas. That was the piece of the address that Leigh hadn't seen but Frank obviously had. That explained why the weapons hadn't shown up any sooner. It'd taken him that long just to locate them.

"How did you find Philip's house?" Gabe questioned.

"I put a transmitter in your car back in Grand Valley. I've been tracking you, waiting for my chance." He glanced down at the blood seeping through his fingers. "Guess I blew it, huh? You win this round."

"It wasn't a game," Gabe told him. He quickly turned to Jinx. "Where's Houston?"

"Nearby. I untied your brother—"

"Philip's here?" Leigh asked.

Jinx nodded. "And with Teresa's help, he should have Jenny and Houston free by now. I told them to wait until everything was over."

Gabe hoped this qualified as everything being over. But it didn't. One look at Frank, and he felt a hatred he hadn't thought he could feel. He realized he still had his gun aimed right at the man.

"I should just kill you," Gabe let him know.

Leigh stepped closer and slid her arm around Gabe's waist. "He's not worth it. When the ATF agents are finished with him, Frank will wish you'd put a bullet in him."

Gabe wasn't so sure about that. He could make things a lot more miserable for Frank than an entire task force of agents. However, he put those thoughts aside when he saw Philip, Teresa and Jenny walking toward them. Philip held Houston, but the boy squirmed to get down. With the exception of his diaper, his son didn't have on a stitch of clothes—Jenny had them in her hand.

Leigh moved at the same time he did, quickly eating up the distance so Houston wouldn't get a chance to see the wounded man lying on the ground. Leigh pulled him into her arms and pressed a flurry of kisses over his face.

"Not a scratch," she relayed to Gabe after she'd checked the child over.

He took his son and did his own inspection, but Houston seemed far more interested in giggling and singing that spider song than he was in his father's scrutiny. Houston pressed a loud, wet kiss on Gabe's cheek and wound his arms around Gabe's neck. It was pretty clear that Houston hadn't experienced any emotional trauma from the kidnapping.

Houston rattled off something that might have been actual words, but Gabe didn't understand him. One look at the child's face, however, and Gabe knew he had indeed understood. Houston smiled, a smile that melted away all the anger and fear Gabe had felt just moments earlier. A smile that touched the very center of his soul.

"Magic, isn't it?" Leigh whispered.

Gabe managed a nod. It was powerful stuff.

He put his arms around his son and wife and held on.

## *Chapter Twenty*

"Well, that's something I thought I'd never see," Jinx remarked after he finished off a glass of ice water.

Leigh made a sound of agreement. Jinx and she were on the back porch of her house and had their attention focused on Gabe and Houston. The Sanchez males were on the flagstone walkway, Houston sitting next to his father. The little boy was trying to teach Gabe how to move his fingers to the now-infamous spider song. With Gabe's large hands, the motions looked absurd. And surprisingly tender.

It made Leigh smile.

"Special Agent Gabe Sanchez, a father." Jinx shook his head. "I wonder if hell really did freeze over. He always said that's when he'd have kids."

Leigh flexed her eyebrows. "Well, I didn't exactly give him a say in the matter."

"Still, he doesn't look upset. He looks content, if you ask me. And happy. Of course, he hasn't actually had to change a diaper yet." Jinx made a sound of mock contemplation. "Let me know when he does so I can give him grief about it."

She was just close enough to send the toe of her shoe into Jinx's shin. Not a kick. More of a friendly jab. "Careful, or I'll pass that chore on to you."

It felt good to joke around with Jinx. Now that the danger had passed, she wondered why she hadn't trusted him. Leigh figured it had something to do with the fact he hadn't kept that conversation confidential they'd had about her pregnancy. Still, she wasn't about to hold that against him.

"What are you two talking about?" Gabe asked. After giving his son a kiss on the cheek, he walked up the steps and dropped down on the porch swing next to Leigh.

"Diapers," Jinx readily supplied. "Hard not to look like a genuine wuss when you're changing a diaper."

"There's nothing wussy about my husband." And Leigh punctuated that with a kiss to Gabe's cheek.

With his dark curls dancing around his face, Houston toddled toward the back porch to join them. His hands bulged with rocks that he'd taken from the flower bed, and she could only guess that he had grand plans for them.

"He sure hates clothes," Jinx commented.

Houston had already discarded his shoes and socks somewhere near the birdbath—after he'd tried to drink some of the water from the somewhat dirty dish. His shirt lay near Leigh's feet. She hadn't even bothered to put it back on him after losing that battle with him twice. The only clothing items remaining were his denim shorts and diaper. She figured the shorts wouldn't last much longer either.

"Does he ever slow down?" Gabe asked, his attention focused on the boy who was busy climbing up the steps toward them.

Leigh grinned and snuggled deeper into the crook of Gabe's arm. "Never." It would be amazing to watch Gabe get to know his son.

Houston made it to them after a few somewhat precarious steps and began to arrange the pebbles on the toes of his dad's boots.

"Well, he sure doesn't look any worse for wear," Jinx went on. "But I was plenty scared there for a while. I can't believe I did something so stupid as to allow Frank to get near the house."

"How exactly did Frank manage to take all of you hostage?" Leigh asked. Since the FBI had only been gone less than an hour, this was their first chance to talk. She hoped Jinx could fill in some of the sketchy spots.

"Because I was stupid, that's why." Jinx shook his head in disgust. "I'd just arrived and didn't hear him come up behind me. He was wearing a ski mask and shoved a stun gun into my ribs. Then he drugged me. By the time I came to, the four of us were already tied up, and none of us knew who'd done it."

That wasn't an image Leigh cared to dwell on so she pushed it aside and concentrated on the rest. "I'm just thankful he didn't hurt any of you."

"And we were lucky that he separated us. I managed to get away while he was checking on the others."

Yes, and that explained why Frank was out in the woods behind the house and why he had that rope in his hand.

"It'll all be in the report," Jinx continued. "But Teresa got Frank to tell her what happened at the house in Grand Valley. Frank wanted to kill you two, but he wanted to make it look like you were just caught up in the wrong place at the wrong time. The two dead men were his hired guns that he eliminated so he wouldn't leave any witnesses."

"But how did he know I'd be on that bridge?" Leigh asked.

"He followed you. Frank was the one who'd been accessing records right and left. He got lucky and located Philip. He said he'd been tailing him for a couple of days before you showed up at the nightclub to tell your brother about your trip. Frank just followed you from there and then apparently accessed the message you'd left on Gabe's machine. That's how he knew you'd be at the lake."

Houston climbed up into Gabe's lap, oblivious to the serious conversation that was taking place around him. He grinned and pinched his father's nose.

Jinx took a deep breath before he continued. "But Frank sure took a chance by following you to that bridge to meet Gabe. Gabe could have seen him. And almost did."

"I've been thinking about that," Gabe explained. "Frank called me just as I was about to leave to meet Leigh. He tried to keep me on the phone, using every stall tactic in the book. Thank God I hung up on him, because my guess is he was already near that bridge waiting for Leigh then."

Leigh pulled in her breath at hearing that. How close she'd come to dying. But it was over. It was finally over.

Jinx got to his feet. "I guess it's time for me to head out. You three probably need some time alone." He reached down and goosed Houston's bare stomach. The boy laughed and wiggled out of Gabe's lap. He returned to his rock-piling activity. "By the way, Leigh, if you ever want your job back, I'm sure that can be arranged."

She hadn't had time to think of anything like that, but it sounded like a good offer. "I believe I'll take you up on that in a month or two. Right now, I really just want to spend some time with these guys."

Jinx nodded. "All right. And Gabe, when I'm gone, you can give Leigh that kiss you've been wanting to give her. Just remember, you've got a pair of little green eyes watching you." He tipped his head to Houston, who was trying to pick grass bits off his blueberry-size toes.

"We'll keep any activity G-rated," Gabe assured him.

Jinx gave them a yeah-right look before he left.

Gabe angled her chin and kissed her. It definitely wasn't G-rated, but at least no clothes were removed.

"I love you," she let him know.

"I love you right back."

The easy way that he said the words brought tears to her eyes. "I can't believe I almost threw all of this away," she whispered.

"I wouldn't have let you do that. Ever."

Yes. She could see that now. What they had wasn't something that could be discarded. After all, she'd fallen in love with Gabe not just once, but twice.

Gabe reached into his pocket and pulled out a ring. But Leigh soon realized it wasn't just *any* ring. It was her wedding band. "I found it on your dresser," he explained. "I thought maybe you'd start wearing it again."

She smiled. "Definitely."

He slipped it onto her finger, adding another of those hot kisses.

Houston pushed his way between them and lifted his arms to be taken. "Up, up."

Leigh reached for Houston, but Gabe beat her to it. He scooped up his son and planted a kiss on the boy's cheek. Houston giggled and slipped his rather dirty, sticky hands around Gabe's neck. The hug he gave his father was hard, long and apparently satisfying to both, because neither of them seemed to be in a hurry to end it.

There was no doubt in her mind that this was right.

She finally had the answer to the question that troubled her. Where would they go from here?

Anywhere.

Everywhere.

Leigh knew it wasn't so much the destination that was important but the fact she'd be making that journey with Gabe and their son.